There was nothing I could do . . .

I saw it coming just an instant before it happened. Time seemed to move incredibly slowly, yet there was nothing I could do to stop it. As Jess barreled down West and plunged into the intersection of West and Stevenson Road, a gold Chevrolet was making its way toward West from the right. She should have seen it; anyone should have seen it. But Jess plunged ahead.

I screamed. Or at least I thought I screamed. I saw Jess twist her head to the right. But it was too late.

"JESS, NOOOOOOO!" I screamed. I hitched myself higher on my bike, doubling my speed. But Jess's scream was already ripping through the air, merging with the long, shrill cry of the car's horn and the screeching of brakes.

Look for these other dramatic
titles from
HarperPaperbacks

Good-Bye, Best Friend

My Sister, My Sorrow

Please Don't Go

Life Without Alice*

* coming soon

The Dying of the Light

Elizabeth Benning

HarperPaperbacks

A Division of HarperCollins*Publishers*

HarperPaperbacks *A Division of* HarperCollins*Publishers*
10 East 53rd Street, New York, N.Y. 10022

Copyright © 1993 by Jan Heller Levi
and Daniel Weiss Associates, Inc.

Cover art copyright © 1993 Daniel Weiss Associates, Inc.

All rights reserved. No part of this book may be used or reproduced in any manner whatsoever without written permission of the publisher, except in the case of brief quotations embodied in critical articles and reviews. For information address Daniel Weiss Associates, Inc., 33 West 17th Street, New York, New York 10011.

Produced by Daniel Weiss Associates, Inc., 33 West 17th Street, New York, New York 10011.

First HarperPaperbacks printing: July, 1993
Originally published by Dell Publishing in January, 1993, as *Jessica's Dying Light* by Jan Heller Levi.

Printed in the United States of America

HarperPaperbacks and colophon are trademarks of HarperCollins*Publishers*

10 9 8 7 6 5 4 3 2 1

For my friends, who saw me through a year of darkness; and for Barbara, too

1

"Madame Picasso-o-o! Yoo-hoo, Madame Picasso-o-o-o-o!"

Before you think I'm an idiot, let me explain. It was a Saturday morning at the end of September, and my best friend, Jessica, and I had a date to go to the mall. But when I got to Jess's house that morning at eleven, her dad told me she was at school. Let me repeat: It was Saturday morning, and my best friend, Jessica Elliot, was at school.

"Let me guess," I said to Mr. Elliot. "In the art studio, right?"

I feel really comfortable with Mr. Elliot. You see, Jess's mom and mine were friends from way back; that's how come Jess and I have been best friends practically since we were born. And then, when Jess's mom died when Jess was four, my folks stayed close with her dad. So she's always over at my house, or I'm at hers, and our parents spend a lot of time together too; it's sort of like one big family in two houses.

"You got it, kiddo," he said. "She said she'd be back by eleven, but I guess she lost track of the time."

I should probably tell you right up front that I happen to be saddled with a perfect best friend. It's not enough that Jessica is incredibly beautiful and smart and funny and talented. On top of all that, she has to go and be the type that actually *wants* to work extra hours at school.

"You know," I confided in Mr. Elliot with a mock sigh, "sometimes I regret that Jess ever talked Ms. Skylar into giving her an extra key to that studio."

"I know what you mean—she's become an addict," Jess's dad said with a laugh. Then little crinkle lines appeared around his eyes. I'd been seeing more of them lately, since he'd been laid off his job at the factory. "Actually, I'm beginning to worry about her, Suzanne. Ever since Ms. Skylar announced that art contest, she's been working herself awfully hard."

I should probably tell you about the art contest, too. At the beginning of the semester, Ms. Skylar—South Somerset High's art teacher and probably the best art teacher in the state of Indiana—announced it over the PA system during homeroom. We were just doing our usual note-passing while our principal, Mr. Whiteman, droned on with the usual boring announcements, when suddenly Ms. Skylar's voice came on, crackling through the static. Right away I saw Jessica perk up.

"I've got some very exciting news," Ms. Skylar said. "I've just learned from *American Arts* magazine in New York that they'll be sponsoring a special contest this year called The Next Generation. Students from more than fifty schools across the country are invited to submit a portfolio of their artwork. A group of judges from New York are going to visit these schools and select the best student artist from each one. The really exciting news," Ms. Skylar continued, "is that Somerset High has been selected as one of the schools. The grand-prize winner from each school will win one hundred dollars. The national winner receives five hundred dollars plus an all-expenses-paid trip to New York to visit museums, galleries, and professional artists' studios. For more details, you can see me in the art studio this afternoon."

I thought Jessica was going to fall off her chair. "Suzanne, did you hear that?" She was trying to keep her excited squeal to a whisper. "Going to New York—it's what I've always dreamed of." Then she tried to get hold of herself. "Of course, I'll never win," she gulped. "Somerset has such a great art program, and I'm only a dinky ninth grader."

Well, whether she was a dinky ninth grader or not, ever since Jess had gotten the details on the art contest from Ms. Skylar, she'd been working in the art studio like a madwoman, even though the judges weren't coming until March 12.

"Even if I don't have a chance at the grand prize," she'd confided in me last week, "maybe I do have a long shot at the school prize. And my dad could use the money," she continued softly.

Now, looking at Mr. Elliot as he ran his fingers through his hair and the worry lines deepened, I wondered if he knew Jess was hoping to win the money to give to him.

"Oh, Jess'll be okay. Don't you worry," I reassured Mr. Elliot—and myself—with a grin. "I'll take care of that. I'm going to drag her off to the mall and make sure she spends the whole afternoon being completely mindless like me."

"Don't sell yourself short, honey," Jess's dad said, looking at me seriously. He smiled. "But I'm glad you girls are going shopping today.

Come on." He grabbed his car keys from the table by the front door. "I'll give you a ride over to school."

So that's how I found myself ten minutes later in the deserted hallways of Somerset High. (Well, not *completely* deserted. There was football practice that morning, and I could hear a few guys laughing and hollering down by the locker room.)

Just in case Jess didn't hear me, or just in case one of those adorable football hunks might have, and wanted to check out the hall to see who it was, I hollered one more time just as I reached the Lincoln Art Studio.

"Aha, Madame Picasso—found you at last!" I announced, flinging open the door.

I'd given her fair warning. Jess whirled around, almost knocking over her easel in the process. She squinted in my direction. "Suzanne, is that you?"

"The one and only. Hey, watch out!" I scooted over in her direction, just in time to steady the still-wobbling easel. "You almost lost your masterpiece there," I teased. "That's no way to win the art contest."

Jess grinned sheepishly. Even with her long hair pinned up haphazardly under a paint-stained bandanna, she looked great. Her green eyes were sparkling. I noticed then, for the first time, this one little misty spot in her right eye, just above her iris. It was like a little cloud that set off the rest of the sunshine in her face.

"Did you forget we have a date to go to the mall?" I demanded.

"Oh, geez, what time is it?"

I pointed to the clock above the door. Her eyes followed my finger.

"Eleven o'clock already?" she moaned.

"Jess," I whined, "try twelve." I regarded her curiously. "You know, I've heard of artists losing track of time, but looks like you've forgotten how to *tell* time."

Jess squinted in the direction of the clock again and mumbled something under her breath.

"What'd you say? What's getting worse?"

"Huh?" Jessica looked startled.

"You said something was getting worse."

"I did?" She scowled. "Uh . . . I was just talking to myself. Anyway, just give me a sec, and I'll be ready—"

"Take your time," I said, sliding into the nearest chair. "I'll just sit here a minute and contemplate your latest artistic triumph."

The art studio is really nice. It's a cheery, high-ceilinged room cluttered with easels, pottery wheels, and paint-stained tables. This afternoon, the sun was streaming in its double-size windows like poured honey.

So I watched as Jessica turned around and peered intently at her painting one more time.

"I just can't seem to get this right," she muttered, rubbing the back of her neck. She'd been doing that a lot lately.

"Jess, are you kidding? Enough is enough. It's wonderful."

It was true, as usual.

On a small table next to her easel, Jess had set up a blue glass bowl and plopped three lemons into it. Pretty ordinary, right? But her painting wasn't. Because nothing that Jessica does is ordinary. Her painting was these three big bold globes of yellow swirls floating in a curl of icy blue. "It looks like those colors just want to burst out of the canvas."

"It does? Does it really?" She turned around to face me. "That's just the feeling I wanted to get." Her face was flushed.

Jess has a way of taking a compliment that makes *you* feel terrific—like it doesn't have anything to do with her at all.

"Yeah," I continued, more slowly now, feeling like the ace art critic of all time, "but why don't you try a little more yellow in the bowl?

7

To get a feeling of the reflection—you know what I mean?"

"Suzanne, you're right! I'm going to try it—" Her voice got a little dreamy as she picked up her brush again, dabbed it in the yellow, and moved it gently through the swirl of blue. I *was* right—the painting looked even better that way.

"I don't know why you don't want to go to New York with me," Jess was saying. She was always talking about moving to New York someday. That's where real artists lived, she said.

"Listen, Madame Picasso, you're the one that's going to go to New York and starve in a garret, not me."

I always teased Jess like that. But, to tell you the truth, I would have loved to move to New York with her, and hang around with artists and writers and musicians. Only problem was, while they were all painting and writing and performing, what would I be doing?

Jess sashayed across the room, waving her brush enticingly. "But it would be so much more fun if we starved together, don't you think?" She plopped down in the chair next to mine. "Anyway, you're not going to starve," she declared. "You're going to go to medical school and become a hotshot doctor, remember?"

Well, it's true—that's what I said once. My mom is a doctor and I've always been good at science and math; that's what gave me the idea.

"Yeah, right," I muttered. Actually, I wasn't sure I had what it takes to be a doctor; it's a *huge* responsibility, making those life-and-death decisions all the time, like my mom does. She's a surgeon at St. Stephen's Hospital; she works in the emergency room a lot. But I figured maybe I could be a foot doctor or something; you don't have to make many life-or-death decisions about bunions, I bet. You just have to look at people's smelly feet all day. Ugh. I decided to change the subject.

"Who do you think will be at the party tonight?" Marianne Massini was having a barbecue party in her backyard that night.

"Oh, the usual crowd," answered Jessica, as she started tidying up around her easel. "Danielle, and Lori and Adam—"

"You're half right," I said, with a sly grin.

"What do you know that I don't know, Suzanne? Come on, out with it."

"Okay. Since we're official high schoolers now, Paul is inviting some of his friends too." Paul was Marianne's older brother, a tenth-grader at Somerset.

"Oh yeah?" Jessica said casually. "That's nice."

I waited.

"Do you think . . ." she started. "Do you think . . . ?"

"What are you trying to say, Jess?" I asked, although I knew perfectly well.

Another silence.

"Oh come on, Suzanne!" she exclaimed. "You know what I mean. Do you think Marc will be there?"

"Marc who?" I said innocently.

"Su-za-anne." Jess waved her brush at me menacingly.

"Oh, you mean Marc Williams? Marc 'Dreamboat' Williams? The guy you got all misty-eyed about after a little chat in the hall the other day? Yeah," I continued matter-of-factly, "he'll probably be there. I think he knows Paul. But I thought you weren't interested in him," I teased.

"Did I say that?"

"Words to that effect," I confirmed solemnly.

"Well, maybe I've changed my mind."

"Oh, really?" I said in mock surprise. For the record, half the girls at Somerset High worship Marc Williams from afar, even though he's just a junior. He's tall and lanky, with gorgeous brown eyes and this absolutely crooked but adorable Patrick Swayze smile. And he's amazingly smart, but not in a geeky way. Marc's a transfer to Somerset High. He just showed up in town last spring. His father is a screenwriter, so he's lived all over the world while his dad worked on different movies. You name it, he's been there—New York, Paris, London.

"But I thought you said he was a snob," I needled her. Actually, my feeling was, if the guy was a snob, he had the right. If I'd lived all over the world like he had, boring old Somerset would definitely seem a fate worse than death.

"Yeah, I did," Jess said, "but after we got to talking for a while, he didn't seem stuck-up at all. Oh no!" Her green eyes widened. "That reminds me. He asked me to do some illustrations for an article he's doing on the new gym. He thinks drawings will be even better than photographs. Guess I'll have to work on that tomorrow," Jessica said. She whipped out her date book—she's the only fourteen-year-old I know that keeps one, but I guess she has to, she's always working on something new—and scribbled down a note to herself in her big loopy handwriting.

That's Jess for you. A ten-minute talk with one of the cutest guys in school and she's already working on a "project" with him.

"Suzanne," she said thoughtfully, as she dropped her date book and purple felt-tip into her backpack, "you know how everybody says it's so horrible to be a teenager, that these are the worst years in your life? I think maybe something's wrong with me." She paused. "The thing is, I'm going to a school that has this great art program, and I've got pretty good classes, and pretty cool friends—"

"And this new interest in Marc?" I added.

"Yeah," she admitted, "that too. The only trouble is my dad's job, and I know he's going to get it back soon, I just know it. And then everything will be perfect for me."

"Shall I alert the media?"

"Come on, stop teasing for a minute. I'm serious."

"You want my honest opinion? Because, in fact, I *do* think there might be something wrong with you. Are you sure you want to talk about this?"

"Yes," she said warily, and her voice went up an octave.

"There is something wrong. Just one thing, but it's really rather serious. If you take care of it right now, there may be hope for you."

It had taken a second, but she was catching

on. "I think I know what it is," she said slowly with mock seriousness.

I nodded. "You're suffering from a very bad case of "mall-deprivationitis—"

"Let me guess the symptoms," Jessica cut in. "One, forgetting that you and your best friend have a date to go to the mall, and, two, keeping your best friend waiting by asking stupid questions."

"Precisely. *Now* can we get going?"

"You got it. Just let me make sure the painting's dry enough to cover." She headed over to her easel again, grabbed a dry brush, and whisked it across the surface of her painting. "Okay," she murmured, mostly to herself, as she gently draped a thin cloth over it. "I'll fiddle with you more on Monday." She turned back to me. "Okay, ready to go at last!"

It's a twenty-minute walk from school to the mall, and on the way there's a place I couldn't live without: Dairy Queen. Someone once told me they don't have Dairy Queens in New York. That's another reason I could never really be happy there.

As we walked, and in between licks of my rocky road cone, I mumbled my assent as Jess plotted a month's worth of activities for us.

"There's this new movie coming to the art theater—we've got to see that! We'll go on two-for-one day to save money—" she began.

"Another one of those foreign films?" I moaned. Last month Jess had dragged me to a movie in Czechoslovakian.

"Su-za-anne." Jess always groaned my name in three syllables when she was impatient. "You've got to be more open to new experiences."

"Jessica Andrea Elliot," I retorted, one-upping her in the syllable department. "Are you trying to tell me that you actually understood that last movie, that you really liked it?"

"Wellll . . ." she began slowly. "Actually . . . well . . . well, no," she finally admitted, dissolving in laughter. "Okay, I admit it, it was pretty horrible. But this one is in English, okay? And I was reading about it in an art magazine, and it sounds incredible."

"All right," I agreed. "I'll give you another chance."

"Great," she said happily, pushing a long strand of golden hair behind her ear. "Then I heard about this cool 'Under the Stars' concert at Thornapple Park next Sunday. We can pack a picnic and go. It's African music. That'll be wild."

Jess went on and on. By the time we got to the mall, she had somehow gotten me into, believe it or not, a discussion of Buddhist philosophy. She'd been reading some book about it, and before I knew it, she was explaining all about things like karma and reincarnation. She told me she thought she'd lived previous lives in ancient Mesopotamia and possibly during the Civil War.

I couldn't decide when I'd lived before. But Jess was convinced I would have been a queen somewhere.

"Dairy Queen, maybe," I said.

She started laughing, and gave me a shove. "Su-za-anne, I'm serious."

"So what makes you think so?"

"Oh, for about a million reasons. But one is because you're so beautiful."

Beautiful? Jess was the beautiful one. Me? I'm okay, I guess. My mom is always telling me I'm gorgeous, but what else is a mom going to say? My skin is nice, it's true, although I'm way too pale. My dark hair is thick and unruly. I've always wished it hung straight down my back the way Jessica's does. I have gray eyes and I'm a little too tall—meaning I'm taller than most of the boys in our class.

Anyway, I may or may not have been a queen

15

in a previous life, but I can certainly shop like a queen in this one. We spent the rest of the afternoon at the mall. I was stockpiling new clothes like Imelda Marcos stockpiled shoes.

It was almost five o'clock when I realized that every package Jess was carrying was one of mine.

"What about you, Jess? Don't you need anything?"

"Oh, don't worry about me," she said. "I've got some remnants from the sewing shop. I'm going to whip up something on my own. But I did notice some tank tops on sale back at Trager's. There was this great fuchsia one in cotton for just seven dollars."

I felt bad. "Hey, let me lend it to you. You don't have to worry about paying me back."

"No, no, that's not what I meant. I've just been looking around for a better buy. But I haven't seen anything. Mind taking a walk back over there with me?"

"Sure, no problem." Still, I felt bad that I had a clothes allowance big enough to buy almost anything I wanted, and Jess had to scout for bargains.

We took the bus back home because I was so loaded down with bags. At one point I glanced over at Jess and was struck by how tired and pale she looked. She was rubbing the back of her neck.

"Are you feeling okay?" I asked.

Her head jerked up in surprise. "Yeah. I'm fine. I just have a little headache—kind of a neck ache, actually. Probably from looking around at all those clothes." She brought her hands up to her temples. "No big deal."

"Are you sure?"

"Uh-huh."

When we got to Jess's corner, she jumped off with her one little package. "Meet you at seven?" I called. "We can walk over together."

"I can't," called Jess. "I'm gonna make dinner for me and my dad. I'll be late. You go ahead without me, I'll see you there."

She waved from the corner as the bus pulled away.

2

I was really excited about this barbecue. The typical party when we were still in middle school was an evening in somebody's finished basement with a CD player. The boys would huddle in one corner, the girls in another for at least the first two hours. Around ten o'clock maybe a few couples would get together for a couple of fast dances; then a slow song would come on, and any girl who was still on the dance floor at that point was probably on her hands and knees on the linoleum searching for a lost contact lens.

But now, like I said, we were official high schoolers, so I was hoping Marianne's barbecue would be different. Especially since an "older man" had been invited. (Needless to say, it didn't occur to me until the last minute that

Paul might be inviting some older girls too.) I'd never paid much attention to Paul, because he'd never paid much attention to me, I guess. After all, I was just his kid sister's ditsy little friend, and he was just Marianne's skinny brother, out shooting hoops in the driveway sometimes when I came over. But Marianne had told me he'd made the soccer team, so I had high hopes for his circle of tenth- and eleventh-grade friends.

Lo and behold, by the time I showed up at seven thirty, there were already a handful of couples dancing on the patio. Another group—both guys *and* girls—was crowded around the grill, laughing and talking. Will wonders never cease?

No sign of Jessica yet. I was making my way over to the grill when I felt a hand touch my wrist.

"Hey there, Suzanne." A pair of slate-blue eyes were staring into mine. "Nice outfit."

I couldn't believe it. "Paul?" I said.

"Yeah. You look surprised. Remember me?"

"Yeah, but—" I couldn't get another word out. I just couldn't believe it. Paul looked completely different. I guess I hadn't seen him over the summer—he'd been painting houses and doing construction with his father. He seemed to have shot up about two inches, and he'd gone from skinny to solid. His sandy-colored hair was streaked lighter by the sun, and his skin was a deep bronze.

"Wow, you look great," I managed to stammer. "I almost didn't recognize you."

"Well, thanks a lot," he said with a laugh. "What does that mean I used to look like?"

"Oh . . . Um . . ." I stammered. "That's not what I meant. I just . . ." Geez. Jess would never have said anything so stupid. She'd be saying charming and witty things. But me, I was tongue-tied. I felt like an incredible dweeb.

"Forget it," he said with a smile. "I was just teasing you. Anyway, you look good too."

After clearing my throat a few times, I managed to squeak out a thanks. "Uh . . . everybody's looking pretty good," I added, trying to recover.

Oh, brilliant. I'd spent hours shopping for this drop-dead peach sundress, these gorgeous sandals that—to tell the truth—were killing my feet, even new earrings and bangle bracelets. Then the first thing I do when an upperclassman talks to me is point out how great everybody *else* looks. My gaze followed Paul's around the yard.

Even if it was stupid, I was right. I wasn't the only one who had done some serious shopping for tonight. Lori Weston was wearing a

21

hot-pink jumpsuit and matching pink-suede cowboy boots that had to have cost a bundle. Danielle Mattick was wearing fabulously faded Guess jeans. And Marianne herself was sporting a to-die-for culottes suit in a wild flowered print that I'd ogled in the designer section of Trager's that afternoon. They were flirting with a group of guys across the lawn, Mr. Dreamboat Marc Williams among them.

"Earth to Suzanne. Come in, do you read us?"

"Oh, sorry, Paul." There was a hint of something I couldn't make out in those slate-blue eyes. Frustration? Boredom? Irritation? Here he was, probably as a favor to Marianne, trying to be nice to one of Marianne's ditsy little friends, and here I was just spacing out.

He drew in a breath. "Aren't you taking French class with Mr. Moseley?" he tried again.

I nodded.

He smiled. "That's what I thought. I spotted you in language lab the other day. I was going to come in, but I was late for soccer practice. Anyway, the way your head was bobbing around, I wasn't sure whether you were listening to French or to your Walkman," he said, laughing.

He was going to come in? To talk to *me*? No,

I must have misunderstood. He'd probably left a book in there or something.

"Yeah," I gulped. "I'd just gotten the new Sinead O'Connor tape, and I couldn't resist," I confessed. *Oh please*, I begged whoever that greater power of Social Life is, *please let me stop blushing*. "I have a feeling," I added, giggling, "that French isn't going to be my best subject."

"Yeah, isn't it a nightmare?" said Paul. "I barely scraped by. I'm taking Spanish this year. Anything to get away from old Moseley."

Oh wow. How come I'd never noticed before the easy way Paul had of shoving his hands in his pockets? Now he was lazily leaning back against the fence that bordered the yard. It was pretty clear he had no intention of moving away.

"I know what you mean," I said. "You'd think the old guy was born talking through his nose like that."

Paul burst into laughter. I couldn't believe it. I'd obviously said something passably witty.

Suddenly, the screen door slammed at the back of the house.

"Suzanne!"

I turned at the sound of the voice—Jessica's voice, of course. And I know it sounds rotten to the core, but at the same time I saw her and was glad that she'd arrived, I also felt this weird twinge of something else. A little sinking feeling, or something.

She looked fantastic, of course. And I wasn't the only one who noticed her entrance. Out of the corner of my eye, I noticed Marc detaching himself from the group of kids he was talking to and moving toward the porch. And almost everybody else's head—including Paul's—swiveled in her direction too, like they were metal filings and she was a magnet. It was pretty much always like that whenever Jessica showed up.

The rest of us could shop our brains out and we'd never match what Jessica could do with a seven-dollar tank top and some imagination.

She'd taken that fuchsia cotton tank top from Trager's and stitched dozens of sparkling buttons of all different shapes and sizes along the neckline. With a few diaphanous scarves floating around her shoulders, and a sarong skirt fashioned out of what I recognized as a stray bolt of curtain fabric from Sew What?—the store where she worked two afternoons a week—she looked like the hippest gypsy you've ever seen. She'd topped if off with three fluttery pastel ribbons twined through her long braid.

So this rainbow comes running down the

steps and across the yard in my direction. And on the way, everyone's calling out to her "Hello" and "Hey, where've you been, Jess? Things were getting boring without you."

But something was wrong. Jess was upset.

She practically skidded to a halt in front of me, and grabbed me by the side of my arms. "Suzanne, I've got to talk to you."

"Sure, Jess. Here? Inside? Wherever you say."

"Inside." She started to tug me along, not even noticing Paul.

"Excuse me, Paul," I said. "Friendship calls."

"Hey, Jessica." Marc appeared behind her, tapping her gently on the shoulder. "What's up? Anything wrong?"

Marc was standing there looking gorgeous.

Jess was suddenly really flustered. I guess she abandoned her plan to take me inside.

"Hey, Marc." I saw her take in a deep breath, then let it out slowly. A smile spread across her face. She seemed to calm down. "No," she said quietly. "I'm okay." She looked around at our concerned faces, and let out another long breath. "Guess I did barrel in here like a ball of fire," she admitted. "But I'm okay now."

We all looked at her suspiciously.

"Really, I mean it, I'm fine," Jess insisted.

She turned to me. "Suzanne, you look great!" she announced. "And to top it off—here!" She pulled off one of her scarves, a filmy aqua one, and whisked it around the neckline of my sundress. She stood back, gave it a tuck here and an adjustment there, then stood back again to admire her handiwork. "I knew this is just what that dress needed when I saw you in it this afternoon! What do you think, guys?"

Marc and Paul nodded their approval, while the God of Social Life, whoever he or she is, refused to let me stop blushing. But Jess was right, and I knew it. I loved the wispy, wafting feel of the aqua scarf floating around my neck, setting off the peach of my sundress.

"Thanks, Jess," I whispered.

She winked a "you're welcome" at me. I told you I had a perfect best friend.

"Now, let's go get a Coke and get ready to dance!" Jess declared.

"But Jess," I whispered, "what is it? What did you want to tell me?"

"You guys go ahead," Jess said, motioning to the guys. "We'll catch up with you."

Jess and I made it halfway to the house when a bunch of the other kids interrupted.

"I'll tell you later," she promised under her breath, a streak of worry crossing her face. "No reason to ruin the fun now, okay?" She had that don't-argue-with-me expression on her face that I knew was not worth contradicting.

"Jessica, what a great outfit!"

"Jess, where've you been?"

"What's up, Jessica?"

Before I could say anything else, Danielle and Marianne and Adam and a bunch of the other kids had surrounded us, and Jess was holding court, joking and laughing.

I lost track of Jess for a while after that. She'd been spending most of her time with Marc, and I had to admit they looked great together—the adorable prep and the wild gypsy girl. It was obvious to everyone that he was crazy about her, and it would only be a matter of time before she'd be the official girlfriend of just about the greatest guy at school. Naturally. Why not? Even as just a dinky ninth-grader, Jess was just about the greatest girl at Somerset High, and everyone knew it. And I wasn't just saying that because I was her best friend, either.

So I was surprised when Jess flopped down on the lawn chair next to mine and asked if she could have a lift home when my parents arrived.

"Sure," I said. "But don't you want to walk home with Marc?"

"Yeah, sure," she said. "But he hasn't said anything about leaving, and it's getting so late."

"Jess, it's only ten o'clock."

"It is?" She looked around, disoriented. "It's so dark, I thought it was later." She giggled. "I guess Marianne wanted a romantic mood."

"Huh?"

"You know, having such dim lights out here."

If you'd asked me, Marianne had gone a little overboard with the strings of twinkly white lights. "Hey, maybe they put a little something in that punch, Jess. You must be drunk. It's lit up like a Christmas tree out here."

"Oh yeah?" Jessica looked even more disconcerted.

"Jess, are you sure you're okay? What's bothering you?"

That's when Paul reappeared with two cans of Coke. "Can I offer you some refreshments?" he asked in grand style. I couldn't help noticing then what a nice smile he had, warm and cool at the same time. Problem was, I couldn't tell if it was for Jessica or for me. I decided to not be picky about it and told myself it was for both of us.

"Thanks," I said.

"I'll pass," said Jess brightly, leaping up.

"Marc's getting me some punch. Think I'll see what's going on with him." She smiled at me before heading off.

"Well, hello again," Paul said, taking the seat beside me that Jess had just vacated. "Guess it's just us."

"Yeah, just us." I was fumbling with the lift-off tab of my Coke.

"Need some help there?" he asked. He took the can from my hand. But rather than opening it, he brought the ice-cold can to my forehead, and rolled it gently back and forth for a second.

I closed my eyes. To tell you the truth, I didn't know whether I was going to faint or die. I figured the latter would be slightly less humiliating.

A new song came on the CD player. "Wanna dance?" Paul asked. Of course, it was a slow song. Most of my slow-dancing experience had been with a pillow. The thing is, pillows don't have toes you can step on.

"Hey, guys, what's up?" It was Marc's voice.

"Go find yourself your own partner, Williams," Paul teased. "We're about to dance."

"Just what I was trying to do," Marc said. "Where'd Jessica go?"

"Went to find you. Over by the punch bowl." I motioned. "How'd you miss her?"

I'm a little confused as to what happened next, because Paul and I were already heading toward the patio. His arms were just circling around my waist, I was just about to melt into his embrace—I swear it was just like in the movies—when all of a sudden there was this loud *clunk!* More like *KER-LUNKK!*—and a lot of squealing and shouting. The music stopped. Everything seemed to stop. Paul released his hold on me and whirled around. The spell was broken.

"Oh, wow!" Across the yard, Marianne was holding out the jacket of her culottes suit and flapping her arms like a sick bird. She was drenched in pink punch. The card table with the punch bowl—and the CD player—was overturned.

As Paul and I headed toward his sister, I could see that a bunch of kids had been splattered, including Jessica.

"Oh, geez, I'm sorry. Sorry, guys," Jess was babbling. "I didn't see the table. I'm so sorry. I guess I lost my balance."

Everybody was saying it was fine, no problem. Marc was already helping to retrieve the CD player and right the table. No big deal, right? Accidents will happen. Only accidents didn't happen too often to Jessica. She was always the life of the party, the center of attention, but not this way.

I guess she couldn't take it. Even though Marc was trying to coax her into wiping off the punch stains with some seltzer and just forgetting about it, she kept standing there, rubbing her hip. There were tears collecting in her eyes. "Really, I didn't mean it. I didn't see the table. I'm sorry."

"Come on, Jess, forget it. Let's dance," Marc said.

"No, I think I'll just head home."

"It's early," I said. "C'mon, Jess, it'll dry. You'll see."

But Jessica insisted.

"Okay," Marc said. "Come on, I'll walk you."

Jessica tried to smile. "No, that's okay, I don't want to ruin the party for you. You should stay."

"No way," he said, grabbing his jacket off the back of a lawn chair and taking her hand. He leaned over and whispered something in her ear. I saw Jess's smile shine through.

"Are you sure you're okay, Jess?" I asked when she came over to say good-bye. "You want me to come along or anything?"

"No, that's okay," she said. She grinned ruefully. "I guess it just wasn't my night. See you tomorrow?"

"You bet," I said. "We've got some talking to do—remember?"

She squeezed my arm, and I held on to her hand for a second. "Hey, Jess, what did he say to you?"

"Huh?"

"You know," I said in a hush. "Marc. What did he whisper to you? I saw you smile."

"Oh," she said, a warm blush spreading over her face. "I think I really like him, Suzanne."

"Yeah?"

"Well, I said I didn't want to ruin the party for him."

"Yeah, I know, I heard that. But what did *he* say?"

Her blush deepened, her voice dropped to a whisper, and her green eyes sparkled. "He said, 'You *are* the party, Jessica.'"

3

Sunday was a total bust. I didn't get to talk to Jessica all day, because my mom and dad and I had to spend the whole day over at Shady Pines—that's the retirement home my grandmother lives in.

But second period Monday, I finally caught up with Jess in the library. We were supposed to be studying for an English test on Emily Dickinson, but there was so much news to report neither of us could concentrate.

"And *then* what happened?" Jess whispered.

I pulled my notebook closer to hers, and tipped it forward to give us more privacy.

"I told you," I whispered back. "Nothing. Absolutely nothing. When they got the CD player on again, it was a fast song, and I didn't see Paul anywhere around. Then, before I knew it, my parents showed up and it was time for me to leave—"

"And he didn't even say good-bye?"

I shook my head ruefully. "I told you—I didn't even see him around. I don't even know if he knew that I left."

"Boys are strange," Jessica whispered philosophically.

"You can say that again," I said. "And what about you and Marc—how was your walk home?"

"Oh, it was nice, Suzanne," she whispered dreamily. "It was *really, really* nice." For a moment, a happy expression overtook the look of worry she'd been wearing all morning.

"LADIES!" barked Mrs. Freeman from the take-out desk. "Are you forgetting where you are?"

It's weird. Mrs. Freeman has a voice like a foghorn. Jessica and I hadn't really been bothering anyone, but when Mrs. Freeman called out, a dozen heads bobbed up.

"Sorry," we mouthed, as we grabbed our books and headed for the hall, sheepishly offering Mrs. Freeman looks of shame as we passed her on our way out.

Once we were out in the hall, I turned to Jess.

"Okay, buster. I've waited long enough. You've got to tell me what was bothering you when you got to the party Saturday night," I ordered. Jess had been looking worried and distracted, and I wanted to get to the bottom of it.

"Oh, Suzanne, it's too horrible to talk about here," she wailed.

"What?" I begged. "What is it? Just tell me. Please."

"I've got to move," she sputtered. "I mean, my father and I—we've got to move."

"Jess, calm down," I said. "What's the big deal? So you've got to move. Lots of people do it."

"No, you don't get it, Suzanne. We've got to move out of Somerset! My father thinks he might be able to land a job in Gulfton. He wants to move right away!"

"Gulfton!" I practically shouted. I thought Jess had been talking about moving to a new house. But this was a different story. Gulfton is almost two hundred miles north of Somerset. "Jess, you can't move to Gulfton! All your friends are here, everything's here. I—*I'm* here! You can't move to Gulfton!"

"I know, I know. I don't want to move! But if it's better for my dad, then I have to."

Now we were both upset. Kids were passing up and down the hall, looking at us funny.

"Oh, great," moaned Jessica, her eyes shiny with tears. "This is why I decided not to talk about it at the party."

"C'mon!" I grabbed her hand and started forcefully down the hall.

"Where're we going?" she asked, running alongside me.

"Someplace we can talk," I said sternly.

A minute later, we were inside the art studio. Thank goodness there was no one in there yet. I made Jess sit down, dab her eyes, and explain everything to me calmly. I sat listening, my arms bent on a desk top, my chin supported by my hands. When she was finished, I sat there for a long minute, not saying anything.

"So, you see," she started sniffling again, "there's nothing I can do. My dad and I have to move—that's all there is to it."

"Shush," I insisted. "I'm thinking."

Silence for another minute.

"Jess," I started slowly, trying to organize my thoughts, "you said your dad doesn't even know whether he has a job in Gulfton yet, right? He just thinks he'll have a better chance there?"

She nodded woefully.

"But the schools aren't anywhere near as

good there as they are in Somerset, right? Everybody knows that. I'm sure your dad does too."

She nodded again. "I don't want to be selfish. Still," she went on softly, "the best art program in the state is right here at Somerset High. I'll never find anything like that in Gulfton."

She didn't even say anything about the contest. But I just knew she couldn't help thinking that she'd have to give up that dream too.

The thing is, I *know* Mr. Elliot. He must have thought about all these things too. He couldn't be any happier about this than Jessica. He probably felt worse.

At first, the idea that was forming in my head had seemed too far-out to consider. But the more I thought about it, the more sense it made.

"Okay," I declared. "What about this. Why can't your dad go up to Gulfton and look around for work while you stay here?"

Jess gave me a long look. "Suzanne, what are you talking about? How could I stay here? We have to sell the house. Where would I live?"

"Well, why does he have to sell the house right away? I mean, that seems like pretty extreme action if he doesn't even know if he's got a real job in Gulfton, doesn't it?"

"What are you getting at?"

"Listen, doesn't it seem a much better idea if you just start out by renting your house here? I mean, that'll bring in money, right? And then," I continued, "then you can come live with me and my folks and finish out the school year here. You know, I bet you by that time your dad will have his job back at the factory, and you won't have to really move at all!"

I realize it's an idea that couldn't work for everyone. But I'm telling you, it actually did make sense in this case. Like I said, my parents and Jess's dad are really close, and my mom and dad adore Jessica.

"Suzanne," Jess said very quietly, "you know, I actually think that might work. I mean, my dad might even like that. But do you really think your parents would?"

"Sure, why not? All we have to do is ask them!"

"And my dad," Jess added thoughtfully. "I have to talk to my dad about it. I don't know, Suzanne. If we did it, I'd miss my dad so much."

"Yeah, I know," I said.

"But people manage to do it somehow . . ." My voice trailed off. Then I had another brainstorm. "In fact, you know someone pretty well who's in the same position."

"I do?"

"Sure you do! Marc!" It was true. Marc's parents were off in Italy for the year, and had decided he'd spent too much time in foreign schools. That's why he'd ended up in Somerset with his aunt and uncle.

"Oh, that's right," said Jess softly, skimming the top of the desk with her hand. "He was telling me a little about it on Saturday."

"Oh yeah? What did he say?"

"He was talking about how his folks call him twice a week, and write to him all the time," she explained. "He says in some ways they get along better this way."

"I bet they do!" I said. "And Jess, your dad would only be a couple hundred miles away. He can come back for weekends, and you can go up there to visit him too. Could be kind of fun."

So now the simple part was done. Jess and I had come up with our plan for the next year of her life. Now all we had to do was get the grown-ups to agree.

"Okay, wipe those eyes," I declared. "And think positively. We just needed a plan, and now we've got one. I'll talk to my parents tonight, and you talk to your dad. Do we have a deal?" I stuck out my hand. Jessica stuck out hers. We shook.

"Let's just hope it works," Jessica said with a sigh as the bell rang and we gathered up our books for our next class.

"It's got to work," I insisted, hoping the confidence in my voice didn't sound shaky.

"I think you're brilliant, honey."

Hurray for my mom! And for my dad, too. I'd just told them the news about Jess and her dad, and the plan we'd cooked up that morning—and they said they thought it was the best idea they'd ever heard.

"Now all we have to do," my dad said, "is convince Hank that it's the best thing for Jessica. I'm sure he'll agree, but he may think he's imposing too much on us."

"I bet you're right," said my mom, sipping her mug of coffee. "You know," she continued, "I bet that's why Hank never said a word to us about this."

"Well, the guy's got his pride, I guess," my dad said.

"Jeff, this has nothing to do with pride. It's about what's best for Jessica. *And* for Hank. Let's go over there and talk with him tonight. I admit it's going to be difficult. No one's got more pride than Hank—except maybe his daughter."

"What?" I said.

"Oh, you know, honey," said my mom, filling her second cup. "Jess and her dad are a lot alike. They're both very independent; they don't like to ask for much."

"But with Jess that's because she doesn't need anything," I responded without thinking. "Why would she? She's got everything."

My mom looked at me kind of funny.

"Everything? What do you mean, Suzanne?"

"Well, you know, she's so talented and smart and great-looking and everything."

"People could say the same thing about you, honey. But you need things sometimes, don't you?"

Like I said, my mom seems to think I'm the greatest. "But it's different with Jess," I insisted.

"She needed you today when she had a problem, didn't she?"

"Well, yeah," I answered slowly. "But *that*'s different." In fact, as I thought about it, I realized that this was one of the few times Jessica had come to me with a problem. I mean, she came to me with lots of other things, but not really with problems.

Anyway, I could sort of tell that my mom was winding up for some kind of lecture (which

41

is also, of course, what moms are for), but I wasn't in the mood. I headed her off at the pass.

"Okay," I said quickly. "So you're going to go to talk with Mr. Elliot tonight?"

My mom and dad nodded. Then my mom checked herself.

"Oops," she said, "can't be tonight, Jeff. I'm on call at the Emergency Room later this evening. But let's call Hank and see if we can get together tomorrow afternoon. Are you free, honey?"

"I think I can get away from the office for an hour or so," my dad said.

"Great. I'm gonna call Jessica right now and tell her we're coming over tomorrow afternoon."

"Whoa there, kiddo," said my dad. "I think this is a talk just for adults. Why don't you and Jessica make some other plans for yourself?"

"Okay," I agreed. "How 'bout twelve bucks for an after-school movie?"

"After that clothes shopping you did Saturday? Forget it," my mom said. "How about some studying? Aren't they giving you enough homework these days to keep you busy?"

"Oh, Mom," I moaned.

"All right, all right," my mom said. "But how about something that doesn't cost money?"

"Oh, that's not my department. I'll have to check with Jess."

"You know," my mom said with a little smile, "it might be really nice to have Jessica around here for a while. There are some habits of hers I wouldn't mind seeing rub off on you."

See what I mean? My mom knows that Jessica is perfect too.

4

When I told Jess that our parents were going to have a powwow the next afternoon and we weren't supposed to be there, she suggested a walk. But as I knew from experience, a walk is never just a walk with Jessica Elliot.

I met her outside Koerner's Drugstore at four o'clock. She was wearing her jeans and a yellow trapeze blouse she'd made herself. She had dozens of pale blue ribbons wrapped around her wrist, and her knapsack slung across her shoulders.

We'd already made a pact that morning. We were both so nervous about our parents' discussion that we promised not to mention one word about it the whole day. We knew it would only make us crazy.

"First things first," announced Jessica. "I

acted like an idiot yesterday, and I'm really sorry."

"What are you talking about?"

"What am I talking about? Try blubbering like a baby in the hallway at school."

"Come on, Jess, you were upset. You act like that's a crime or something."

She shook her head. "It's the second time this week I've acted like a total idiot. First, I splash everyone with punch at Marianne's party and then—"

"Cut it out," I said. "So you got upset twice—big deal. Geez, when I get PMS I cry if someone looks at me funny. You don't always have to act so together, Jess. Maybe it's good for you to shed some tears every once in a while. Everybody does it—"

"Thanks, Suzanne," she said softly. Then, with renewed determination in her voice, "But it's not something I'm going to make a habit of."

"Jess—"

"All right, all right, enough said." She started walking toward Oxford Street.

"Okay. So where are we going, and what's the meaning of those ribbons around your wrist?" I asked.

"You'll see." She smiled. "Come on."

We headed down Oxford Street and turned

onto Main. In Somerset, late September is still mostly summer, with just the best hints of fall. Jessica knew the names of all the trees. Serviceberry, hackberry, black walnut, butternut—they're all pretty much the same to me. But not to Jess.

We turned left on Sunset, the road to Thornapple Park.

"It's hard to imagine," she muttered, "that Thornapple Park was once the center of town. Then when they brought the railroad through at the other end, everything gradually shifted over there."

"How come you know all this stuff, Jess?"

"I've told you a million times," Jess said with a smile. "You have to pay attention to everything around you if you want to be an artist. It isn't enough just to lock yourself in a studio. You have to go out and see things, find out about things."

"Too bad there's not much to see in Somerset," I said.

"But there is! A whole lot more than in Gulfton, I bet."

"Jess!" I put my finger to my lips. "We promised not to say a word about that. Now stop it, you'll jinx our plan."

"Okay, okay. We'll talk about something

else." She looked thoughtful for a moment. "Yesterday we talked about our past lives. Let's talk about our future ones today, all right? You start."

"What am I supposed to say?"

"Anything you want."

"Okay," I declared firmly. "I'm going to marry Paul Massini."

Jess raised an eyebrow in surprise.

"Hey," I was quick to say, "I just picked his name out of a hat."

"Right," she said, laughing. "Go on."

"Okay, so where was I? Oh, that's right. At the altar with Paul Massini. But I'll retain my maiden name, of course—for professional reasons."

Jess nodded her approval. "*Dr.* Welch."

"No, I've changed my mind about that. I'm going to become an exotic dancer and work at the roadstop out on Route 27. I am going to have to call an end to my career, however, after Paul and I have our seventh, eighth, and ninth kids—triplets named Paul Jr., Paul the 3rd, and Little Paul—because I've gotten so fat."

"How fat? Fatter than Roseanne Arnold?"

"Roseanne Arnold will be svelte compared to me. I'll then go to work, temporarily, in the circus. This promising career will be cut short, however, when they find a fat lady even fatter than me."

"What are you going to do then?"

"Oh," I said blithely, "probably then I'll go on the Slim-Fast diet, divorce Paul after many happy years together, leave him with the nine kids, and go become a doctor. Either that or compete for spokesmodel on Ed McMahon's *Star Search*."

"An excellent plan," said Jessica. "I do think you'd have a gift for stroking appliances on game shows."

"Thank you," I said. "And you?"

"Well, naturally, this artist thing is just a silly adolescent phase. My true dream is to become a dental hygienist. Really, I can't think of anything more fulfilling, more thrilling, than day after day, week after week, scraping the plaque off of endless people's choppers."

"Oh, Jess, that's just the half of it!" I swooned. "Think of the joy of scheduling appointments for root canals, operations for gum disease. I truly envy you."

"Maybe I'll let you come in from time to time and wash the crud off the drill."

"How generous of you! I'm at a loss for words. And where does Marc Williams fit into this scheme?"

"Oh, he's the dentist, of course."

"Uh-huh. I get the picture. So you'll marry the boss."

"Perish the thought! He'll be a dentist with a free spirit, and I'll be a dental hygienist with an equally free spirit. We'll just live to-gether—like Simone de Beauvoir and Jean-Paul Sartre, like Lillian Hellman and Dashiell Hammett."

"Come on, Jess," I whined. "Who are they?"

"Oh, you know. Famous unmarried couples," she said. "Like, um . . . Sam Shepard and Jessica Lange."

"Oh, I get it," I said. "How romantic!"

"I really like him," said Jess, getting serious.

By this time we'd reached Thornapple Park, and the edge of Thornapple Lake. Jess clamped her hands over my eyes.

"Okay, you've never seen this place before, never even seen a place *like* this before. Okay." Jess released her hands and jumped back. "Now what do you see? Come on," she coaxed, "you know the rules, say whatever comes into your head, it doesn't matter."

Her face looked so happy and carefree I had to smile. This was a game we played all the time when we were little.

"All right, but this stinks. I'm out of practice," I complained. "Um . . . let's see . . . A pool of silver, okay?"

"A pool of silver, a pool of silver." Jess rolled the syllables over her tongue like she was tasting them. "Not much, but it's a start," she decided.

As we circled the lake, Jess and I took turns describing it with whatever words popped into our heads. Soon we let go of the lake, and just let images tumble out of our mouths. It didn't matter if they made any sense. This was always the way the game went.

"The finger of a butterfly!" I said.

"The last blossom of a dogwood in April!" she said.

"The sky between the stars!" I said.

"Now we're beginning to roll." Jessica clapped her hands. "Come on!" She sprinted ahead, toward a hill of brush overlooking the lake. I raced to catch up with her.

"Hey, Jess," I called after her disappearing figure. "Not another climb up to Sutter's Point!"

"Expect the unexpected!" Jessica's voice floated down.

Okay, she had something up her sleeve. I sprinted after her. It's true we'd made the climb to Sutter's Point before. Everyone knew that at the top of this footpath that sliced through the trees, you came to a flat sheath of rock that gave you a pretty good view of the west side of town.

But I'd never taken quite this route before. I raced after Jess, following her path through the thick brush by the blue ribbons Jess dropped.

Suddenly, about twenty yards up, where the path heads off to the right, and just a few yards before you reach Sutter's Point, a blue ribbon dangling from a bush told me that Jessica had veered left. It was harder going now, steeper, and the brush was thicker.

"Wait a minute," I called, huffing.

After about ten more yards, I hit a little clearing and found a new ribbon leading me up. From here on, the trees and brush thinned out, and the air grew cooler. It felt like the clean smell of the trees was surging right into my lungs. Suddenly, I heard Jess's voice again.

"Over here!" she yelled.

I broke through the last sentry line of small blue fir trees. The hill opened out onto a curved grassy field. There were no more trees, just blue, blue sky all around us, and this incredible view of the softly rolling hills and meadows that make up the dairy farmland stretching east of Somerset.

Jess was standing at the edge, with her back to me, her blond hair blowing in the breeze.

"How come I never knew about this?" I said when I came up beside her.

"Because we always follow the path," Jessica said simply. "I was hiking up to Sutter's Point the other day with my sketch pad and journal. But it was so crowded when I got there; there were a bunch of kids drinking beer. And then I realized I'd always followed the path, and I wondered why. That's how I got to be here."

"Hey, look," I said. "You can see all the way to Ridgeley Farm. See, Jess, see the writing on the side of the silo?"

But Jess just stood there quietly, a vague smile playing across her face.

After a bit, I fell silent too. We just stood there a minute, enjoying the breeze in our faces. Then she broke the promise again, but I didn't care.

"I don't want to leave Somerset, Suzanne," she said so quietly. It was quieter than a whisper.

I didn't know what to say. That's when I noticed the faintest music.

"Hey, what's that music?"

Jessica tossed her head in the direction of her knapsack on the ground behind us. Beside it was her small tape player. I don't know what kind of music it was exactly: a little bit of flute dipping in and out, and piano. Maybe there was some violin in there too, and some guitar. But it didn't sound like instruments at all; it sounded like a melody you'd always known, but never heard before.

"Come on," Jessica said. The wind picked up her hair, then settled it down softly on her shoulders as we grabbed the tape player and headed toward a soft patch of grass at the lip of the promontory. Jess knelt down and turned the music up just a drop. Then she lay down on her back in the grass, gazing up into the sky.

"Come on, " she beckoned, talking into the sky. "Real dreams, this time," she said.

I lay down on my back beside her on the soft grass and gazed into that blue, blue sky.

We didn't talk. We didn't need to. The song changed. Now it was just a single breath of flute weaving in and out of the blue. The clouds passed over our heads in soft, rich puffs.

Two dopey high-school kids flat on their backs on the top of a hill. To someone who had come along and seen us, we probably would have looked stupid. But it didn't feel that way.

It felt wonderful.

When I think of everything that's happened since then, and especially what's happened to my friend Jessica, sometimes that afternoon, the two of us lying down on the side of that hill dreaming about I'm not even sure what, seems like a dream itself.

5

"Jess?" I was down on my hands and knees with my nose stuck deep in my closet. "Have you seen my brown shoes? I can't find them anywhere."

I felt a slap on my behind. "Hey! Ouch!" I squealed. I backed out of the closet and sat on the floor, looking up at her with accusing eyes. "What'd you do that for?"

"Because it was there." Jess grinned impishly. "And no, I haven't seen your shoes. But it's no wonder. The way you throw your clothes all over the room, it's a miracle you can find anything. Why can't you be more organized, like me?"

With that, she jumped off the side of one of the beds in my room—excuse me, *her* bed, *our* room—and opened the closet on her side.

There, hanging in an orderly row, were her dresses, skirts, and blouses. Beneath them, her three pairs of shoes tidily faced us, toes pointing out.

"You know," I said, "if you were really my friend, you'd mess that up a little. You're really giving me a bad name around here," I pouted jokingly.

Well, I guess you've probably figured out that Jess's and my plan had worked. Her dad had bused it up to Gulfton two weeks before with some job leads.

After Mr. Elliot had thanked my parents about a thousand times, and after my parents had said there was absolutely nothing to thank them for about a thousand times, we all saw him off at the bus station. Then we stopped at Jess's house to pick up her stuff and move her over here.

In a way, because our folks are so close, Jess and I had always been kind of like cousins. Now, with her living with us, we'd become more like sisters. Before we did pretty much everything together; now we did *absolutely* everything together. Including tearing my—I mean, *our*—room apart looking for my brown leather slip-ons, since we were going to the movies that night.

"Found them," I hollered, reaching behind

my bedside table, where the shoes were crammed amid some forgotten Kleenexes, candy wrappers, and about a dollar and a half in change.

"I can't hear you!" Jess sang out from the bathroom.

"I said," coming to the door, and regarding my best friend perched in front of my vanity (a great hand-me-down from my grandmother), "I found them."

"It's a miracle," Jess clucked. When she spotted me in the reflection from the mirror, she quickly dropped her hands to her sides.

I came up behind her and put my chin on the top of her head, so both of our reflections gazed back at us. We grinned at one another in the mirror.

There was Jess, with her shining blond hair, tan skin, and delicate features; and me, with my splash of almost black waves, wide mouth, and pale, pale skin. Could there ever be two girls who were closer yet more different? We were practically opposites—and not only in looks.

She was the let's-jump-in-deep-water-and-see-how-we-swim type; I was the let's-dip-our-toes-in-the-shallow-end-and-get-used-to-it kind of girl. She was a wild orchid, I thought, and I was your everyday black-eyed Susan.

"Paul's not really interested in me," I announced, for about the hundredth time that evening.

"Suzanne," Jess said impatiently, giving me an elbow in the ribs. I grabbed a blush from the vanity table, straightened up, and started dabbing it on my cheeks.

"Why do you keep saying that? I didn't notice Paul hesitating to make it a double date when Marc asked me to the movies tonight."

"That's true," I conceded. "But . . ."

"But what?"

"But," I said, snapping closed the blush compact, "I don't think he would have asked me if Marc hadn't asked you first. I think he just wants to come along for the ride, and I happen to be the most convenient extra passenger."

"That's ridiculous," said Jessica. "What are you saying—that Paul really wants to be around me and Marc?"

"No . . . not exactly. . . . I mean . . ." The problem was, I didn't know what I meant. I thought that maybe Paul did kind of like me, but that maybe he found me a whole lot more fun to be with when Jessica was around. And frankly, I couldn't blame him. But how would I explain that to Jessica? I just kept hemming and hawing.

While she was waiting for me to put my thoughts together, her hands went back up to her face again. She was kind of fussing with her eye.

"Got something in your eye?" I asked.

Jessica's hands flew down to her lap again. "No," she snapped sharply. Then she noticed my look of surprise at her tone.

"Sorry," she said quietly. "But listen, Suzanne, I know Paul likes you."

"Oh yeah? And how do you know?"

"I just . . . I just . . . well, I just know, that's all," declared Jess, thumping her hand on the vanity.

Before I could probe her psychic powers any further, my mom's voice floated up from downstairs. "Girls, your dates are here!"

Jessica raced down with her usual exuberance, and flung her arms around Marc. You'd think she'd feel real strange doing that in front of my parents, but she was so genuinely enthusiastic that everyone, including my folks, just seemed to understand it. "I spent the whole afternoon in the studio," she said, her voice filled with energy, "and I'm almost finished with this sculpture I really love!"

"That's great, Jess," Marc said, giving her a look of total admiration and devotion.

I'd reached the bottom of the stairway now, after trying for a graceful, sophisticated descent that no one particularly noticed.

"Hello there," Paul said with a nice smile, but I still felt like a pale shadow of Jessica.

"Now you kids have a nice time," my dad said. "And go ahead out for some pizza after the movie if you want. But if it gets too dark to walk home, I want you to call me, understand?"

"Yes, sir," said Marc.

"Thanks, sir," said Paul.

"Sir," my dad repeated ruefully, turning to my mom. "I never thought I'd be a 'sir.'"

"I know, honey," my mom said, smiling at him in commiseration. "Time sure flies when you're having fun, huh?" She turned to us. "Now, you kids have a good time and behave yourselves, okay? Us old folks are just going to stay home in our rocking chairs and count our gray hairs."

My dad groaned.

Once we were on the road, I began to feel a little—just a little—more confident.

Jess and Marc were walking ahead of us, so it was just Paul and I together. We started joking together about the movie we were going to. Because, believe it or not, Jess had talked us all into going to the one playing at the art theater she'd told me about.

Well, I have to admit it, it was really a pretty good movie. Not a lot of laughs exactly, but still a good movie. It was a documentary about an artist that Jessica really admired named Frida Kahlo. She did these really strange and incredible paintings. And the story of her life was even more incredible.

She was in a freak bus accident when she was young. She was really badly hurt. Her spine was broken and twisted in about a million places, and she lived the rest of her life in constant pain. She had to have more than thirty operations, and none of them really did much good. She had to spend one whole year flat on her back in bed, but she had her friends and her husband—this fat but kind of sexy artist named Diego Rivera—fix up some sort of contraption over her head so she could paint while she was lying down.

The thing was, even though she was really messed up physically in a zillion ways, she never gave up on her work. And she still managed to live this incredibly exciting life, with lots of lovers and everything.

Wow—pretty heavy stuff. Like I said, not a lot of laughs.

Actually there was one thing that happened

that really made us laugh. It was pretty dumb, but we were in kind of a silly mood, I guess. Marc and Paul were behind us, carrying the mesquite-flavored popcorn (remember, this is the *art* theater in Somerset) and Jessica was leading us through the darkened theater in a big hurry because she was so anxious to get us good seats.

"There!" she pointed, "there are four right there. This is perfect!" Before I could stop her, she was already halfway in the row.

"Hey!" yelled this irritated voice. "What're you, blind? What do you think you're doing?"

At the same time I heard Jessica squeal, "Oh wow, I'm sorry!" She dropped her pocketbook and everything spilled out of it, clicking along the floor under the seats.

It turned out there was this big guy sitting in that seat, his dolled-up girlfriend sitting right beside him, and Jessica had plopped herself right down in his lap!

Marc and Paul and I were hysterical. Jess was mortified at first, but then she started laughing really hard too. It took us about ten minutes to collect all the stuff of hers that had rolled under the seats, right through the coming attractions.

Then Marc took the lead and we quickly found four seats together—unoccupied.

Anyway, the rest of the evening was pretty

fun. I stopped worrying about whether Paul really liked me, because we were having such a good time together.

I'm not going to tell you about the goodnight kiss I got at the door, because that's personal, but I will tell you that it was fairly dreamy.

Anyway, I must have teased Jessica about that seat fiasco on and off for about the next two weeks. In fact, I was probably teasing her about it that afternoon in the art studio when she was just putting the finishing touches on her new sculpture. I couldn't help it. She'd just finished another wonderful piece. It was a wood figure of a woman, her arms raised into the air in a kind of ecstatic pose, like she was reaching for the sky. It was really pretty amazing. Plus, Jessica was still managing to put in two afternoons a week at her job at Mrs. Morgan's Sew What? and *still* get home in time every so often to actually make dinner for my folks and me. And she never failed to make my mom and dad laugh all the way through the meal at the funny, interesting stories she told. Frankly, it was getting to be a little much.

So, anyway, like I said, we were in the art studio, and maybe I had been teasing her a little too much, so I switched the subject. "Worried about your competition for the art contest?" I asked.

I didn't figure she really would be—she was so good—but we couldn't help seeing that there were some pretty good things around. Some really good photographs, for example, by a junior named Sam Wendover. And a bunch of excellent watercolors by a girl named Jorie Campbell. They were small pictures of flowers. They looked almost good enough, I thought, to be professional illustrations. Her violets really looked like violets, her roses like roses. In spite of my loyalty to Jessica, I was impressed.

Jessica looked around the room. "Some of this stuff is great," she said. "There are a lot of talented artists in this school."

"But you're the best, Jess."

"Oh, I don't know." Her eyes looked tired as she idly rubbed the back of her neck. "I wish I could work harder and get a few more things finished up to put in my portfolio. But I keep getting these stupid headaches. And neck aches, too."

I gave her a puzzled look. "Like the one you had the afternoon of Marianne's party? When we took the bus back from the mall?"

"Uh . . . yeah, I guess," she said. "Sometimes

I wish we had eyes where our ears are."

"Huh?"

"You know, it gets tiring, doesn't it, when you're really concentrating, to keep having to turn your head all the time to see things?"

"I don't know, I never really thought about it. I guess you're right. But I don't get neck aches from it. Not that I noticed, anyway. Maybe you need glasses."

"No!" said Jess so sharply I was startled.

She flushed, and her voice softened. "Sorry," she said. "I just know I don't need them, that's all."

"Do I detect a note of vanity, my friend? Afraid you won't look good in glasses?"

"Of course not. It's just that I—"

"Come on. I think you'd look ravishing in some of those thin wire rims. Really artsy, you know?"

Jess smiled, but her brow was furrowed. "Glasses aren't cheap, Suzanne. I can't bug my dad long-distance now with any extra expenses."

"Yeah, but this is your health!" I said. Then something in Jessica's expression made me ask, "How long have these neck aches been going on?"

"Oh," Jess said, "not so long."

"How long is not long?" I persisted.

"I don't know."

I looked at her skeptically.

"I don't know," she said firmly.

I had a feeling she wasn't telling me the whole truth.

"But you've had them at least since September, right?" I asked.

"Oh, I guess. Kind of off and on. Anyway, forget it, it's not important." She started talking about our French homework, but I interrupted her.

"What about the that at the movie? Does that have anything to do with this?" Suddenly what had seemed so funny then didn't at all now.

"No, that's something else," she said quickly. Then she caught herself. "I mean, no," she said forcefully. "Listen," she snapped, "aren't you ever going to let up on that? That could happen to anyone, Suzanne. It's like you *want* something to be wrong with me. Come on, cut it out."

You can bet I shut up after that crack. Because the worst thing was, maybe Jessica was right. Maybe I was just looking for any little thing that would prove to me she wasn't perfect. So I let it drop.

*　　*　　*

The following Sunday, Jess and I were studying for our first real high-school midterms. We were up in *our* room, with books and papers sprawled across the beds.

"Mr. Moseley's French is going to be the death of me," I wailed.

"Here, let me help you." Jess grabbed my verb book and started putting me through my paces, and correcting my accent.

"If the letter's there, why don't they pronounce it?" I complained. "It's so stupid."

"Su-za-anne."

"I know, I know, 'I've got to open myself up to new experiences,'" I recited in a singsong imitation of Jessica. "Well, I'm sorry, I don't want to open myself up to this new experience. No one speaks French in Somerset anyway."

I guess it goes without saying that Jess was doing really well in French. That's because, as she always told me, she not only wanted to live in New York someday, but she wanted to spend her summers in the south of France. Give me a break.

"Hey, Suzanne, can you go through some of the geography assignments with me for a minute?" Jessica asked, after I had made it clear that my brain would not accept one more French verb.

"Sure," I said, completely surprised that Jess was actually asking for my help on something.

And I was even more surprised to discover, as we went through it, that she hardly remembered anything.

You see, Jess was always a great student. In French and everything else. That's why I was really surprised to discover she was doing badly in geography.

Everyone knows geography is an easy-A course. All you have to do is just stare at whatever map Mr. Vickers happened to pull down that day and listen to him drone on about major crops, bodies of water, and stuff like that while he tapped it with his pointer. So it was completely bizarre that Jessica couldn't remember anything for the test.

After unsuccessfully trying to jog her memory with my notes, we went back to studying our own books in glum silence. But something was bugging me. "Hey, will you move the shade on that lamp or something? It's like a spotlight."

Jessica moved it, about one hundredth of an inch.

"Jess," I complained. "Come on, it's making a glare on my books."

She could really be stubborn.

I stood up and pulled the shade down abruptly. "There, that's better." I climbed back on my bed.

A second later, she'd inched it back up again. This was really getting annoying.

"Hey, what's with you?" I barked.

She gave me this really strange look. "Well, I need more light to study, sorry."

"More light? Jess, it's lit up like a Christmas tree in here."

Wait a minute. Dejá vù. You know what that is? When you say or do something, and all of a sudden, you have this feeling like it's happened before, but you can't explain where or when. But I *could* explain it. I had actually said those words before. And to Jessica. Then it came back to me—the night of Marianne's party, when Jessica had been saying how dark it was in the yard.

"All right, I've had it." I jumped off my bed, scattering papers across the floor. "I'm going down to talk to my mom right now. You need glasses, buster."

"No, Suzanne. Please . . . don't." Jessica was off her bed and clutching me by the arm. "It's nothing, really," she stammered. "I—I mean, I'm used to it and—"

"You're used to it?" I repeated, not quite

71

sure why I was repeating the words, but sensing something.

"You know, at night, sometimes, that's all . . ." Her voice trailed off.

Something flashed into my head. Six months ago, Jess had sprained her right wrist. Most kids decorate their casts with other kids' signatures. Not Jess, of course. She'd shown up every day with something different. One day her cast was covered with a collage of famous masterpieces clipped from art magazines; the next day it was the score of the *William Tell* Overture dancing around her arm; Memorial Day it was an American flag sling.

"Jess, how did you break your wrist last spring?"

"Oh God." Her giggle cut through the tension for a minute. "You'll never let me forget that one, either, will you? Okay, here we go again. It was Danielle's slumber party, and I got up in the middle of the night and walked smack into her bathroom door and fell down hard."

"Exactly, Jess," I said as gently but as decisively as I could. "You've been having trouble with your eyes for a while, haven't you? You've got to do something about it. You've got to tell my mom. She'll make an eye doctor's appointment for you."

"Suzanne, pul-ease—it's nothing, really. I'm sorry I mentioned it, okay?"

"Don't be sorry. You've just got to do something about it," I insisted.

"Okay, okay," she said. "But not tonight, all right? I've got so much to do now, with my job and the contest and studying for midterms. I promise if it doesn't go away by Christmas break when my dad comes down, I'll talk to him." She brightened. "He's going to get me a Christmas present, anyway, right? So who knows? Maybe I'll end up with a pair of glasses."

I contemplated this for a moment. It was just the beginning of November; Christmas was kind of far off. But then again, Jess was probably right. Though I knew her dad would love to give her something more than glasses for Christmas, he still didn't have a permanent job up in Gulfton—he was doing day work through an agency. So glasses might be all he could afford.

"Okay," I finally agreed.

"Thanks, Suzanne. I knew I could count on you."

She went over and adjusted the light as best she could so it didn't cast as much of a glare my way, and we went back to our studying.

A few minutes later, she lifted her head, reached over, and gave me a tap on the arm.

"By the way," she said coyly. "Do you really think I'd look good in those wire rims?"

"Quit fishing for compliments, four-eyes," I said, tossing a pencil at her.

6

It was the following Wednesday, November 5, that it happened. We'd just sweated our way through two days of midterms, and, wouldn't you know it, Jess was back in the studio, furiously working. It took me forever to coax her out of there to meet Paul and Marc at the *Somerset High Signal* office.

We'd all ridden our bikes to school that day, because Jess had decided we could show the guys our special view near Sutter's Point before it got too cold.

We met them, gathered up our bags and sweaters, and were passing by the art studio on our way out of school. I could see Jessica slowing her pace. We all knew what was coming.

"Just for a minute, please? Just to take one last look, I promise," Jess pleaded.

"There's no such thing as just a minute when you disappear into the art studio," I said.

"But if you guys go in with me, I promise it'll just be a minute. You can drag me out if I try to stay. I promise. Come on, please," she whined playfully. "I'll have much more fun if I just can take one look at my sculpture before we leave."

We couldn't argue with that. Now I wish we had. I really wish we had.

The shades were pulled down in the art studio, and since it was late afternoon, and the studio is on the east side of school, it was pretty dark. But Jess didn't turn on the light. She just barreled into the room, eager, I guess, to check up on her work.

The thing is, someone must have moved her piece. I saw it—it was just to the left of the door on a pedestal—but Jess didn't. She was heading across the room when her elbow brushed the side of the pedestal. Jess's ecstatic lady wobbled back and forth for an instant, then clattered to the floor.

"Oh no!" Marc gasped.

Jessica whirled around and made a choking sound.

Marc immediately flicked on the light and joined Jessica on the floor, where she was kneeling by her sculpture. He reached under a nearby desk and pulled one brown arm of the sculpture out from beneath it.

I was too stunned to do anything.

Fumbling, he held it to the figure, as though it were a puzzle, and this was a piece that could hopefully be glued back in.

"It was all one piece," Jess choked. "It was all one piece of wood." She was shaking. "I worked so hard on her. How could this have happened?"

"Oh Jess," I gasped.

"Come on, let's find Ms. Skylar. Maybe it can be fixed," Paul volunteered.

"No point. It's ruined," Jess said flatly, climbing to her feet. "Listen, Suzanne, you take the guys on the ride. I—I'm going home," she said in a rush.

She broke away from Marc and was out the door before we could stop her.

"Poor Jess," I said. "She was really proud of that piece. She thought it was her best thing so far."

"I know," Marc said. We all looked at one another helplessly for a minute.

"Listen," I said, jumping up. "I'm going to follow Jess. We'll do the bike ride another day."

I ran out of the room and through the front entrance of the school.

By the time I got to the bike racks, Jessica was already pedaling out of the parking lot on her beat-up Raleigh. I hopped on my ten-speed Schwinn, and started after her at a pretty fast clip.

But Jessica picked up speed as she made the wide turn onto West Street. Her hair was streaming out behind her like yellow ribbons. She ducked her head like a racer, and zoomed into the wind, her legs pumping furiously.

I knew what she felt like; when you're so upset you just want to move as fast as you can, so fast that your feelings can't catch you.

I saw it coming just an instant before it happened. Time seemed to move incredibly slowly, yet there was nothing I could do to stop it. As Jess barreled down West and plunged into the intersection of West and Stevenson Road, a gold Chevrolet was making its way toward West from the right. She should have seen it; anyone should have seen it. But Jess plunged ahead.

I screamed. Or at least I thought I screamed. I saw Jess twist her head to the right. But it was too late.

"JESS, NOOOOOOO!" I screamed. I hitched myself higher on my bike, doubling my speed. But Jess's scream was already ripping through the air, merging with the long, shrill cry of the car's horn and the screeching of brakes. I flung my head to the side just before the impact. I couldn't bear to see it.

"Oh, my God!" a deep voice bellowed. A car door slammed. I looked straight ahead again and kept pedaling. The driver was stumbling toward Jessica. She was sprawled in the middle of the street. Her bike must have been catapulted by the impact, because it was twisted in a heap over by the curb. Its front wheel was still spinning round and round and round.

"I couldn't stop in time, I couldn't stop!" the driver was hollering, as I screeched to a halt beside Jessica. There was blood everywhere. "Don't touch her," he insisted. "She's breathing, but we shouldn't touch her. Call an ambulance!" He gestured frantically toward the phone booth just up the street. He started fishing in his pocket for some change.

"I'll call 911," I said in a shaky voice, and took off.

Please God, let her be all right, let Jess be all right, I prayed to myself as my trembling fingers punched the digits on the phone.

"911 emergency line. What's the problem? How can we help you?"

"Please," I sobbed. "There's been an accident! My best friend! There's been a terrible accident!"

7

mother weaker Jessica." Two nurses were already at the foot of the gurney. "We'd gotten So very much blood," said and I—well there were about a hundred things going on...

Jess was lucky. At least, that's what we all thought at first.

My mom zoomed out of the glass doors of the emergency room as the ambulance pulled up to St. Stephen's. She pulled me close to her while she barked out instructions to the paramedics. (We were really lucky: They'd radioed ahead, so my mom not only knew about the accident, but knew it was Jessica coming in.)

"Are you sure you're okay?" she asked, still clutching me tight as she leaned over Jessica's gurney. Jess was still so pale, breathing in little choking rasps, and there was blood all over her face.

"I'm fine, Mom," I wailed. "But please help Jessica, you've got to help her!"

"I will darling," she said, releasing her hold, and racing alongside the gurney as the paramedics wheeled Jessica in. Two nurses were already at the door to meet the gurney. "Workstation Six," my mother yelled, "and IV—stat!" There were about a hundred things going on at once, and my mom was the one leading it all.

"Suzanne," she yelled over her shoulder as she disappeared behind some white curtains with Jessica's gurney. "Go sit down in the waiting room. Someone take my daughter to the waiting room," she instructed, and before I could say a word a nurse detached herself from the group and had me by the arm, leading me away.

"Come on, honey," she said. "Your mom is going to take care of your friend, don't you worry."

"I want to stay with her!" I cried. "I've got to!"

But it was no use; the nurse just kept moving me away. She got me into the waiting room and pointed to the house phone. "Use your mom's code." She recited the three numbers. "She wants you to call your dad at work and ask him to come over here. He'll know what to do after that. And if you need anything, honey, or you get scared, you can just talk to Mrs. Raymond over there." The nurse pointed to a gray-haired lady bent over a pile of forms at the reception desk.

It seemed like hours before my dad arrived, and several more before my mom came from the Emergency Room. But it was probably only about twenty minutes.

"She's going to be fine, honey," my mom said, pulling off her surgical gloves and shoving them into the pocket of her smock. "She's got a couple fractured ribs, and she took a nasty blow to the head. That's why there was so much blood. But she's really going to be okay. We've called in Dr. Wendell to do a little procedure, and then . . ." Her voice trailed off. "Now I want you and Dad to go home and have some supper; you may even be able to come back and see Jess tonight."

"Jake Wendell?" my dad asked. "What's he going to do, Shelley?"

"Suzanne, you sit down for a minute. I want to talk to Daddy." She pulled him aside, and they stood there whispering for a minute or two.

When my dad came back, he told me he was going to call Jess's father from my mom's office while she went back to check on Jess. "Wait here, honey. I'll be right back," he said.

"I want to come with you."

"No," he said slowly. "I want you to wait here."

"Dad, what is it? What's wrong? Mom said Jessica was going to be okay!"

"Honey, we've got to call Jess's dad right away. If you were in the hospital in Gulfton, don't you think we'd want to know?"

"Yeah, but—"

"There might be a little complication. Your mom wants Dr. Wendell to check it out. And Jess's dad has to give us permission to okay any, um, procedures that might be necessary."

"What kind of procedures?" I started feeling like I was going to cry again.

"Suzanne, honey, calm down. It's not worth worrying about until your mom checks it out."

Dinner was horrible. I just kept pushing the food around on my plate while in my mind I went over the accident again and again.

"I should never have let her run out of that studio alone," I told myself for about the millionth time.

My dad reached across the table and put his hand over mine. "Stop it, Suzanne. Stop blaming yourself. This isn't your fault. Let's try to have a positive attitude until we hear from your mom."

But I couldn't help noticing he hadn't touched a bite of his food either.

When the phone rang, I jumped up to get it. It wasn't my mom, it was Marc, whom I'd completely forgotten about. He flipped when I told him Jessica was in the hospital. He remembered hearing sirens, but he never dreamed they were for Jess. I repeated what my mom had said, that Jess was going to be okay. And I promised to call after I had more news about when we could visit. But as convincing and comforting as I tried to be, the memory of my parents' expressions as they huddled together in the waiting room kept haunting me.

"Dad," I said softly, after hanging up the phone. "What kind of doctor is Dr. Wendell?"

He looked at me in silence for a moment.

"I mean there was really a lot of blood on Jess's face," I continued nervously. "She's not going to be"—I could hardly choke the word out—"she's not going to be, you know, *disfigured*, or something?"

"Honey, I really don't know much more than you do. Now come on, eat your dinner. We'll hear soon enough."

My dad was on the phone with Mr. Elliot in the bedroom when my mom walked in. She looked really tired.

I was up on my feet in a second and pound-

85

ing her with questions before she even had a chance to take off her coat. "How is she? Can I see her? What did Dr. Wendell say?"

"Honey, we have to talk." She pulled off her coat and sat down beside me at the kitchen table. She was still in her hospital smock, her stethoscope still hanging around her neck. And her face was so serious. When my dad came in, my mom smiled up weakly at him, then gestured toward another chair.

"Hank's taking the next bus out of Gulfton. He'll be here by midnight."

My mom nodded.

"Shoot," he said softly, "we're waiting."

I looked beseechingly at my mother.

"Suzanne," she said, taking my hand, "things are a little more complicated with Jessica than we originally thought—" She broke off in midsentence and brushed her hand through her hair.

For some reason, I couldn't bear to look in her eyes. I just kept staring at her stethoscope, a small disk of silver slowly swinging back and forth, catching and losing the light like a blinking eye. I couldn't take my eyes off of it.

My mom began talking again. I heard the words, but I didn't want to absorb them. They went around and around in my head like heavy marbles, one hitting another, another hitting a third, the third hitting the first, and the whole dull cycle repeating itself until I thought I would scream. Anything to get those words out of my head.

Retinitis pigmentosa. Retinitis pigmentosa. Jess had something called "retinitis pigmentosa." My mom explained that these cells in her eyes—the cones and the rods that "receive" the impulses and send them to the brain, which makes the picture—were degenerating. She said the progress of the disease is really unpredictable, that often a person's eyes deteriorate over the course of several years. But the impact to Jessica's head in the accident had jostled her retinas, and the weaker cells had torn. Dr. Wendell, who it turned out was an eye surgeon, had done an operation to correct that. But given the condition of her eyes beforehand and the fact that they had already been deteriorating for a year or two, it was likely that she had lost a good deal of sight anyway. Within the next several months, she could be, for all practical purposes, blind.

"Well, fix it!" I blurted out. "What's the cure?" I felt like I was choking.

"I'm afraid there isn't any cure, honey. Not yet, anyway. Maybe scientists will come up with a cure someday, but right now, there's just not much we can do. Except help Jessica cope with this."

"I don't believe it!" I screamed. "How could this happen! How could I let her ride off like that? I knew she was upset!"

"Darling, stop it, stop it," my mom said, taking hold of my hand. "Retinitis pigmentosa is an inherited condition; the accident didn't cause it."

"Inherited? From whom?" I demanded.

"Honey, it develops in different people at different times," my mother explained. "Dr. Wendell thinks it's highly possible that Jess's mother might have developed retinitis pigmentosa if she'd lived longer."

"Anyway," my dad said, taking my other hand, "that accident wasn't your fault. And none of us had any idea that Jess was suffering from this."

"That's right," my mother said wearily. "We had a chance to talk to Jessica about it before she went into surgery. She admitted that she'd been having some serious problems with her eyesight for quite a while. She said it had been getting harder for her to see things to the right and left without actually twisting her head. That's probably why she didn't see the car; she doesn't have normal peripheral vision anymore; she has what we call 'tunnel vision.' Anyway, she was scared, so she'd been hiding these things from everybody. Hiding it from herself, too, I think," my mom added with a sigh.

"I knew." The words fell out of my mouth like dead things.

"What did you say, Suzanne?" My mom reached out and pressed her fingers gently to my chin, raising my head.

The tears were burning my face.

"I knew," I said again.

Then I told them about the conversation Jess and I had just a couple of days ago, the things I had noticed in the past few months, and even what I suspected about her bumping into the bathroom door and breaking her arm at Danielle's slumber party.

"I just thought she needed glasses!" I wailed. "But I should have made her tell you the other night. And I didn't, I didn't!"

My mother pulled me into her arms, and started rocking me like I was a baby. "Shhh, shhh," she said over and over. I couldn't stop crying. "Suzanne," she was crooning gently, "you misunderstood. There were lots of warning signals of this disease. If we'd known what they were, we would all have done something. Even Jess. And the things that seem obvious to us— well, they look obvious now, but they didn't then." She leaned back and looked gravely at me. "And you have to accept, honey, that this disease just runs its course no matter what any of us does or doesn't do. I know that's the hardest part for us, in a way."

"Can I see her?" I asked timidly.

"Of *course* you can see her," my mom said. "But not tonight. Visiting hours are over and, in any case, Jessica needs her rest. But tomorrow, okay? How's that?"

"Okay," I said weakly, blowing my nose into the paper napkin she'd offered me. "I've got to call Marc. I promised."

"Why don't you let me call Marc. And if Paul calls, I'll explain things to him too," my father suggested. "I think the best thing you can do now is get some rest, sweetie."

I knew I really should have called Marc, but I was relieved that my dad said he'd do it.

"That's right," my mom said. "And when you wake up tomorrow, Jess's dad will be here, and you can see Jess, and we'll start . . ." Her voice trailed off.

My dad picked up. "And we'll start dealing with this thing," he said. He smiled at me. "Because we're gonna get through this. All of us. Together."

Lying up in my room—*our* room—with

Jessica's bed empty beside me, I stared into the dark. *This is all Jessica will be able to see*, I kept telling myself, and the tears would start again. Jessica. Blind. Jessica. Blind. The words just didn't go together. But it was true. It didn't matter what anybody said or did, Jessica was going blind.

8

"See what happens when you get too in-volved with your artwork," Jess joked, tapping the white bandages that covered her eyes. "At least all I did was run into a car; Vincent van Gogh cut off his own ear!"

I attempted a lighthearted laugh and so did Marc, who was sitting stiffly in a chair next to me.

"I can't wait to get out of this creepy place," Jess continued. "It's incredibly boring. All they let you do is lie around. And with these ban-dages, I can't even watch TV. Soap operas are twice as dumb, believe me, when you can only listen."

It had been three days since the accident, three days since Jess had been told about the retinitis pigmentosa. But she was still acting like once she bounced out of that hospital bed, everything was going to be the way it had always been.

"Sounds okay to me," I said, trying to make my voice sound normal. "Want me to change places with you? You can go back to school, and I'll just lie around in here listening to old *I Love Lucy* episodes.

"It's a deal!" Jessica brushed aside her sheets and dangled her slender legs over the side of the bed. "Marc, grab my coat and I'll be out of here." But in mid-laugh, she fell back and pressed one hand to her ribs, the other to her eyes. "Owwww," she moaned softly, wincing.

"Jessica Elliot, what do you think you're doing?" My mom was standing at the door with another doctor. He was maybe forty, and a major hunk. His eyes were light blue and really friendly looking, and he had coffee-color wavy hair that looked a little windswept, like he'd just come off the ski slopes or something. "Haven't I told you to stay in that bed unless a nurse was here?"

"Sorry," Jess said weakly as my mom went over and tucked her in again.

"Jess, I've brought someone to meet you."

"Hello, Jessica," said the handsome hunk, striding across the room and taking her hand in his. "I'm Dr. Graham and I'm very happy to meet you. I've heard a lot of wonderful things about you from Dr. Welch."

"Dr. Graham," piped up my mom, "this is my daughter, Suzanne, and Jessica and Suzanne's friend, Marc Williams."

Dr. Graham reached over to shake our hands and smiled warmly at both of us.

"Jessica," my mother began, after settling in an orange plastic chair and stretching out her legs, "Dr. Graham is the director of Hope House, and he's hear to talk to you about your going there for a little while. Maybe Marc and Suzanne can go get a soda while we talk." My mother shot me the "scram" look.

But before I could move, Jessica was waving her hands. "Stay here, guys," she instructed Marc and me. "I told you," she said firmly to my mother, "I'm not going to Hope House." She bobbed her head a little vaguely, trying to figure out, I guess, where Dr. Graham was standing, then settled for facing just a little to the left of her bed. She couldn't know that Dr. Graham had quietly moved aside and taken a seat next to my mom. "Thank you for coming, Dr. Graham," Jessica said courteously, "but I really don't need to go to Hope House. So you're kind of wasting your time."

"What's Hope House?" asked Marc.

Only someone who hadn't lived in Somerset very long would ask that. You see, Hope House is probably the most famous place in Somerset. It's this special medical center just for kids, set in this beautiful old Victorian mansion. People say it feels a lot more like a home than a hospital. Kids come from all over the place to get treatment there. It's even been featured on shows like *60 Minutes* and *20/20*.

I began to explain this to Marc, but his face seemed to sort of shut off.

"You mean like a Ronald McDonald House, something like that?" he interrupted me. "They have one of those in L.A."

"Well, not exactly. But something like that," Dr. Graham broke in. "The lucky thing for Jessica is that Hope House is right here in town. She can check in for a few weeks while she's recovering, get some counseling, and begin learning some of the sightless skills she's going to need in the future."

I could see Jess frowning and shaking her head, but Dr. Graham cheerfully plunged ahead. "Then, if things go well, she can be back in school in a few weeks, and just visit Hope House from time to time as she needs us."

He turned to Jess and saw her expression.

"So what do you have against the idea, Jessica?" he asked gently.

Scram, my mother's look insisted again. I motioned to Marc, and we slipped out.

"I don't think she should do it," Marc blurted once we were out in the hall. "Jessica doesn't belong in a place like that."

"Yeah, that seems to be what she thinks too."

"Well, she's right," Marc insisted. "Those places are creepy. You won't catch me walking into one of those joints. My sister—" He broke off, swallowed hard.

"You have a sister? I didn't know that. Is she—"

"*Had* a sister," Marc said flatly.

"Huh?"

"I said '*had* a sister.' She's dead."

I just stared at him for a second.

"She's dead, Suzanne. Get it? *D-E-A-D,* dead. She died in one of those crummy children's hospice places in L.A. She went in there to get better, and she came out dead."

"What was it?" I said in a whisper.

"What's the difference?" He looked down at his hands. "I was twelve years old, she was sixteen. I thought she was the greatest. She *was* the greatest. In fact," he paused and cleared his throat, "when I first met Jessica, she reminded me of Dana."

"You never said anything," I said softly.

"What am I supposed to say? 'Hi, I'm Marc and I had a really great sister who's dead now, and by the way, what's your name?'"

"I'm sorry, Marc," I said quietly. "I'm really sorry."

We both just stood there for a minute. I guess neither of us knew what to say.

Then I broke the silence. "Listen, Marc. Jess is going to be okay. This thing isn't going to kill her. Going to Hope House would be different for her than for your sister. Jessica's really strong. She can beat anything."

"That's what I thought about Dana too," Marc mumbled. He looked up and met my eyes for the first time. "There are different ways of dying, Suzanne. Some of them don't even kill you. My sister had brittle daibetes since she was a baby. People say that you're not supposed to die of diabetes, but she had some kind of kidney complication. She went blind about three months before she died. She was stumbling around all over the place; she couldn't even go to the bathroom alone. It was so awful."

"Marc—"

"Forget it, Suzanne. Listen, I'm late. I gotta get home for dinner. Tell Jessica I said good-bye. I'll . . . I'll . . . maybe I'll talk to her tomorrow—"

He shoved his hands in his pockets, turned, and headed down the hall with his shoulders hunched over. He didn't look back.

"She won't do it. She won't even hear of it," my mom said. She was fixing herself a drink, something I hadn't seen her do since I broke my leg in seventh grade. My dad and Jess's dad were sitting on the couch in our living room. Mr. Elliot was bent over with his elbows on his knees, cradling his head in his hands.

"I don't know what I'm going to do," he said, his voice muffled. "I've still got my health insurance coverage from the factory—thank God for that. But just when things were looking up . . ."

That was the ironic thing. The day before Jess had her accident, the factory where he'd worked had announced that they'd be rehiring the laid-off workers come May. That meant Jess's dad would have his job back, and they wouldn't have to move for good. But it was only November and he'd just landed a five-month temporary assignment in Gulfton that was going to tide him over. Now, with Jessica's accident . . .

"We've discussed that, Hank," my father said, gently but firmly. "You're going to finish out that stint in Gulfton; you can't walk away from that money. And Jessica is going to stay here with us. If she won't try Hope House right now, so be it. We'll find a way to make this work until you can get back here permanently."

"That's right, Hank," agreed my mother. "I know you and Jessica have talked about it too. She understands completely."

"But if she won't go to Hope House, maybe I should take her with me. It's too much to ask of you all."

"Hank, I understand how you feel," my mom said, taking the smallest possible sip of her drink. "But that won't help at all. In fact, taking Jessica away from Somerset now—away from the school she's familiar with, away from the friends she knows—would make things much more difficult. Think about it."

My dad turned and nodded at me. "Suzanne's the best thing for Jessica now; she can help her in a hundred ways here, and at school. Aren't I right, honey?"

I nodded. Of course he was right. But suddenly I felt scared. Me help Jessica? It had always been the other way around.

Two days later, Mr. Elliot and I went to pick up Jessica at the hospital. The bandages had come off, except for a little white patch over her right eye.

"Pretty exotic, huh?" she said.

They made us take her downstairs to the front entrance of the hospital in a wheelchair, even though Jess protested.

When her dad went to get the car, Jessica reached up over her shoulder and tapped my hand. "Have you seen Marc around lately? I haven't heard from him."

"Uh, I think he's been pretty busy, with the newspaper and all. He'll probably call once you get home." I tried to make my voice sound normal.

"Oh," Jessica said with a little intake of breath. "Yeah, I'm sure you're right. Who wants to hang around a creepy hospital and see your girlfriend wrapped in bandages? I think it gives him the heebie-jeebies. I'll see him at school."

"Yeah, right," I mumbled. What else could I say? Marc had practically disappeared since that day when he'd told me about his sister.

I was pushing Jessica around on the sidewalk, trying to entertain her, when Dr. Graham passed by on his way into the hospital. He stopped and came over to us.

"Jessica," he said, "I'm glad to see you're going home. And remember what we discussed. Anytime you think you might want to come to Hope House, or even if you just feel

101

like talking, you give me a call, okay?"

"Thanks, Dr. Graham," Jess said stiffly, rising out of the wheelchair as my mom and dad pulled up in the car. She smiled brightly. "But I'll be just fine."

When we got to our house, I came around the side of the car to open Jess's door and help her out.

"Su-za-anne," she said curtly, brushing my arm aside. "Cut it out. I can do fine on my own."

And she could, she really could. She marched up the walkway to our door without a false step. Perfect as usual.

That march up to our front door was about the last time I saw Jessica do anything perfectly. Not that she didn't keep trying. But the more she tried, the worse things got.

That first week alone, she bruised her shinbone badly when she walked into the ottoman in our living room, burned her hand on the stove because she couldn't see that it was on, and cut three of her fingers when she knocked over a glass and tried to sweep up the shards herself.

School was even more horrible.

"Jess!" I called to her her first day back, catching up with her in the hall outside English class. "You left your glasses at home." I pulled them out of my bag—these special, heavy, thick-framed contraptions they'd made for her at the hospital.

"I don't want them," she said. "I'm fine."

"Jess, you've got to wear them. They're supposed to help. Come on, put them on."

I didn't really blame her for resisting. The glasses really were horrible. When she put them on, her eyes looked like they receded about a million miles. She didn't look like Jessica at all; it was kind of spooky.

It was all so strange for me.

Just a few weeks ago, I'd been getting really fed up with Jess always being the perfect, beautiful, bubbly, wonderful one, and me being the gray shadow next to her.

But now, suddenly, she couldn't be all those things, and I felt even worse. I didn't like seeing Jessica this way. It made me feel lonely and scared. Like she'd deserted me, somehow.

To top off the awkwardness of that afternoon, Marc walked by. Jess saw him, or sensed him maybe, and from his expression I could tell he wished she hadn't.

"Oh, hi, Jessica. Hi, Suzanne. How ya doin'?" He looked like he didn't want to wait around for the answer.

"Just great, Marc," Jess said brightly. "Except for these hideous things Suzanne keeps trying to put on my face. They're really gross. I hate them."

She dropped them into her bookbag and zipped it closed. "How are *you* doing?"

"Oh," he said, not looking up. "I'm fine." He just stood there a minute, looking like he was trying to put some words together, explain something. "Uh, listen," he said finally. "I've gotta go. I'm going to be late for history."

"Okay," Jess said. "See you around."

"Yeah, well, maybe I'll . . . I'll call you sometime, okay?" Marc said as he walked away.

"Yeah, okay," Jess called back softly.

But he didn't. Call, I mean. Not that night, or the next night, or the next night, or any night. That didn't mean the phone wasn't ringing. It was, plenty. Paul. For me.

Life is truly ironic. And tragic.

Just as Jessica was losing everything, all these things were happening to me. Things that would have seemed really wonderful at a different time.

It made me feel very strange. Paul and I were getting closer and closer. I really felt comfortable and happy around him now, but I felt guilty about Jess.

"How about a movie Saturday night? The new Mel Gibson?" Paul asked one Thursday evening after we had been talking for a while. My hand holding the phone began to feel kind of sweaty.

"The new Mel Gibson? Uh, sure. What about Jess?"

"What about her?"

"Well, I don't like to think of her sitting home alone."

"Suzanne, I care about Jessica too, and what's happened to her. But you can't be with her every minute!"

He was right. Of course he was right.

A month before, I'd have been sure Paul would have dumped me like a hot potato if it weren't for the reflected glow Jessica cast around me. And now, things weren't progressing with him because I felt too nervous about leaving Jess behind.

"Paul," I pleaded. "I know, I know. But just let me ask her, I mean—"

But I didn't have to. Jess was passing by the kitchen, and she must have heard me.

"Are you trying to get Paul to drag me along with you on another one of your dates?" She grabbed the phone away from me. "Paul? Hi. Listen, you've got to get this girl out of my hair." There was a pause. "No, thanks. Thanks for asking. But I'll be fine. Besides, I don't even like Mel Gibson."

"Jessica Andrea Elliot," I declared, stomping into our room a few minutes later.

She was lying on her bed, the lamp turned high, squinting at an old book of pictures by Frida Kahlo she'd taken out of the library.

"You're a big liar," I said. "You love Mel Gibson."

"But I don't love being a third wheel."

"You're not a third wheel. We'd love to have you—"

"'We'd love to have you,'" Jess repeated in a high-pitched, fake-sounding voice. "Get off it, Suzanne, you're really getting on my nerves," she snapped.

I couldn't believe it. After all I'd done. I really wanted to let her have it.

But I checked myself. God, Jessica was sick. She was going blind. How could I even think of yelling at her?

I chose my words carefully, and tried to keep my voice nice and easy. "It's okay, Jess. Don't worry about it. Listen, can I get anything for you?"

Jess pulled back her arm, and the Frida Kahlo book came flying at me at about a million miles per hour. I had to duck, or I would have gotten it in the face.

"'Jessica, can I do this for you? Jessica, can I do that for you?'" She was using that high-pitched fake voice again. "'Jessica, would it help if you sat closer to the blackboard?' 'Jessica, would it help if you sat farther from the blackboard?' I'm sick of it!" she shouted. "I don't want to hear it anymore. Marc is the only one that's honest—at least I'll give him that!" She was practically screaming. "I don't want your help and I don't want your pity, Suzanne. Just leave me alone, and I'll get along fine. I always have and I always will!"

I couldn't help it. I burst into tears. But angry tears.

"You think this has been fun for me?" I shouted back. "You think I like this? You're so busy pretending that everything's the same, that you're still perfect Jessica Elliot, the girl who can do everything. But you can't! You're not perfect anymore, Jess, and you can't stand it! So you're taking it out on me. But it's not my fault!" I yelled through my tears. "It's not my fault your stupid eyes weren't made right! It's not my fault this whole thing happened! But I could handle it if you'd just be honest about what's happened, if you'd just accept it. But no, not you! You can't stand to have any weaknesses!"

Jess just stared at me, her face growing paler and paler.

"Jess," I cried, feeling awful about my outburst. "I'm sorry, I didn't mean it."

"Yes, you did, Suzanne," she said hollowly. Her face looked pinched and as white as chalk. "Now, if you're finished, do you mind if I get some sleep?" She leaned over and switched off the light.

"Jess, I'm so sorry, really," I moaned into the darkness.

"It's all right, Suzanne," she said, her voice sounding so flat it scared me. "Go to sleep."

I slunk out of the room and changed into my pajamas in the bathroom. When I crept back in, I tried one more time.

"Jess?" I said softly.

I could tell she was awake, but she wouldn't answer me. I slipped into my bed and pulled up the covers.

When I woke up in the morning, Jess wasn't in her bed.

Not in the kitchen either when I went down for breakfast.

"Jess go out?" I asked my mom casually, bit-ing into an English muffin. My mom didn't show any signs of having overheard our fight, and I didn't want to tell her about it if I didn't have to. I figured I'd talk to Jessica today, apologize again, and we'd make it up.

"Suzanne, Jessica had a little accident last night," my mom said.

My heart dropped to my toes.

She explained that Jess had gotten up to get a drink of water at about two in the morning. But she'd slipped and fallen down the stairs.

I don't know how I'd managed to sleep through it.

"Is she all right? Did she really hurt herself?" I asked.

"No, thank God. But she could have."

"Where is she?"

"She's at Hope House, Suzanne. I checked her in there early this morning."

9

"I'm sorry," a kind but firm voice told me, "but Jessica isn't taking calls from anyone today."

"But I'm not just anyone," I insisted. "I'm her best friend. Did you tell her it was Suzanne?"

"Yes, honey," the voice answered patiently. "I told her that, just like I told her that yesterday and the day before."

I hung up the phone.

"Still no luck?" my mom asked quietly.

I shook my head and sank down on the stairs by the landing.

"What am I gonna do, Mom? How can I make it up to her if she won't even talk to me?" I had finally told my mom all about the fight, and it had felt good getting it off my chest.

111

"Suzanne, **honey**," my mom said gently. "I think there's a **whole** lot more going on here than your fight with Jessica."

"But she hates me now, Mom. She really hates me."

"No, I don't think she hates you at all. I think she loves you very much."

"This is some way of showing it," I said miserably.

"Suzanne, this is a very, very difficult period for Jessica. Maybe she just needs a little time to get her thoughts together, you know what I mean?"

I wasn't sure I did. How could I figure out what Jess was feeling? I couldn't even figure out what I was feeling.

Two days later, I got the letter. Here's what it said:

> *Dear Suzanne,*
>
> *I've thought a lot about what you said to me the other night, and I'm writing to tell you that you were right. Not about everything. But about some things.*
>
> *I was so busy thinking about myself that I didn't think about what this thing was doing to you. You're right. It can't be fun for you. Because I'm not the old Jessica,*

and I'll never be able to be her again.

Since I've been here at Hope House, I've thought a lot about what it means to go blind. Because you were right—I wouldn't let myself think about it before. But here's what it means, Suzanne.

Being blind means someday soon I won't be able to see the sunset or the sunrise. Someday, not so long from now, it will always be midnight for me, and a midnight without a glowing moon or a single star. It means I won't be able to see my dad's face, or your face. And you know how, after you haven't seen someone for a long, long time, you start to forget what they look like—you can't picture their face in your mind's eye? Well, it means that too. It means that someday I won't even be able to remember exactly what you or even I once looked like; I won't even have that to comfort me.

I know blind people can walk, of course, with canes and Seeing Eye dogs. But they can't walk like I've walked.

Remember the day I took you off the path to Sutter's Point, and we came upon that wonderful view, the one I'd found when I went exploring? I'll never be able to do anything like that again. Already, they're teaching me here how to concentrate on memorizing the placement of things around me, taking things slow, moving deliberately. When things gets worse, I'll always have to walk the paths and the routes that are familiar to me.

I won't be able to dance, because I might knock into something and hurt myself. I won't be able to read, except books in Braille. I won't be able to go to the movies, the circus, play tennis, go bike riding, learn to drive.

People always say, "Well, sight is only one of the five senses, and isn't it kind of wonderful what happens to blind people? How their senses of hearing and touch and smell and taste become so intensified that they notice things we don't?"

But Suzanne, have you ever thought about how much of our life is seeing? How can you smell or hear or taste a sunset, a beautiful painting, or a face you love?

It's not like in the movies, Suzanne. Blind heroines are always beautiful and smiling bravely through it all. I guess that's what I was trying to do. But once I got here, I started thinking about it more. I once knew someone blind; my great-aunt Bess went blind from glaucoma when she was seventy—

and I don't remember ever seeing her smile. I remember asking my dad about it when I was a kid. He thought about it for a while. Then he said he thought maybe it was because my great-aunt couldn't see people smiling at her, and even if she did smile, she couldn't be sure that her smile was really reaching anyone. You see, Suzanne, even smiling is in the eyes.

And then there's my art. A blind artist—it's a contradiction in terms. Even though I'll still be able to see pictures in my mind, I won't have any way of knowing if I'm getting them into the painting or the sculpture or the drawing. I won't see colors anymore, won't know which ones to choose, and whether a line should go here or there, because I won't be able to see where here or there is anymore.

I'm sorry I blew up at you the other night. But you can't imagine what it feels like not being able to be Jessica anymore. Instead, I'm just a girl who's going blind. I know people mean well, I know they're trying to help, but you can't imagine what it's like. My eyes have been bad for a while, Suzanne, worse than I let on even to you. Maybe that was stupid, but I'm not so sure. Because now that everyone does know, and know it's going to get worse, they have changed toward me. They talk in these sweet, pitying tones; sometimes they even talk about me like I'm not there. "Should we do such-and-such for Jessica?" they say, like I'm not even standing there. And then there's Marc. He ignores me completely now, but even that is better than pity.

The old Jessica was your best friend, Suzanne, and you were her best friend. I used to be fun to be with, at least I like to think I was. And I never had so much fun as I had with you. It hurts so much to not be able to be that Jessica anymore. And I feel that pain the most when I'm with you. I feel like I'm letting you down and letting me down too. So will you please do this one thing for me? It's the only thing I'm going to ask you, so please promise to do it for me. Don't answer this letter, don't call me anymore. Just let me put my life back together again and become the person I'll have to be.

I've asked Dr. Graham if I can live here at Hope House until my dad comes back to Somerset, and he said okay. I realize that must sound pretty strange considering how stubborn I was about coming here, but I've accepted the fact that I really belong here now. I guess I'll start going back to school at some point, and when I do, I know we'll run into each other and say hello and stuff, but let's not do anything more than that. I want to be able to remember our friendship—and I want you to be able to remember our friendship—the way it was. I want you to be able to remember me the way I was.

That's the only thing I'm asking you to give me. It's the only thing I can give you. And if you think about it, you'll know I'm right. I'll miss you so much. I already do. And I know you'll miss me. That's the way it should be. But the only way I think I'm going to get through this is by starting new, and the same for you.

But don't ever think that I'm angry with you, or don't like you. And please don't hate me for this. I couldn't bear thinking you hated me. You were the greatest best friend that a loony bird like me could ever have. I only hope I gave you as much as you gave me.

Good-bye, Suzanne.

> So much love from your old friend,
> Jess

10

Two weeks turned into three, and Jessica still hadn't come back to school. Kids asked me how she was, and I answered as best I could. She'd begged me not to call or write, and I hadn't. I found out about her only through reports from my mom, and from Jessica's dad when he came down to visit.

One day I ran into Marc as he was coming out of the *Signal* office. "Hey, Suzanne," he said awkwardly.

"Hey, Marc," I said, shifting my books in my arms.

"Uh, what's new?"

"Nothing much."

There was a long awkward silence.

"You and Paul ever get up to that place she showed you?" he suddenly said out of the blue.

"You know, the place we were going to ride to that day . . ." His voice trailed off.

"Nah," I said. "It's too cold. Anyway, I just don't feel like it."

"Yeah, I know what you mean." That adorable Patrick Swayze smile was kind of pinched. I felt sorry for him, I really did. I guess he couldn't help it if Jess reminded him of his sister who died.

"Yeah, well . . ." he picked up again. "Guess I'll see you around."

"Yeah, see you around, Marc."

It was a Saturday morning. Jess's birthday. Her dad was coming down later in the day.

It had snowed the night before. The ground was still covered with white, and the tree branches looked dark and lacy against the gray sky.

As I left the house, I didn't tell anyone where I was going, just hopped the M13 bus to Hope House. I decided to walk the last ten minutes of the trip. It was so quiet I could hear the crunch of my boots in the snow.

Hope House is at the end of a row of other beautiful Victorian homes. It has a big, wide porch wrapping around it, and lots of bay windows with shutters painted yellow.

I climbed the steps to the porch—it had been swept clear of snow—took a deep breath, and rang the bell. The door was answered by a friendly-looking black woman about my mom's age, I guess.

"I'm Suzanne Welch, a friend of Jessica Elliot's."

"Oh, Dr. Welch's daughter! Well, come in, Suzanne. You must be freezing. I'm Nurse Hayes. Welcome to Hope House."

She hustled me inside, into a large airy front room with a grandfather clock, thick patterned rugs on the polished wood floors, and three or four comfy-looking overstuffed armchairs.

"Take off those wet things and make yourself comfortable," she said, pointing to the closet.

Before I could answer, a bunch of kids came into the room, laughing and yelling. They were hanging all over a lady in a nurse's uniform who had silvery gray hair piled up on top of her head. She was teasing the kids, and they were loving it. When she spoke, I could hear a hint of an Irish brogue in her voice.

The lady who had answered the door went behind a desk near the window and wrote something down on a clipboard. I went over to her. "So you're here to see Jessica, is that right?" she asked. "Let me tell her you're here."

"No, that's okay. I don't think Jessica will

see me." I pulled a heavy package wrapped up in bright pink paper out of my shoulder bag. "I just wanted to leave this here for her. Will you tell her it's from Suzanne?"

It was a big new art book. It had cost me about three weeks' allowance, but I had to do it. It was about Frida Kahlo and had lots of gorgeous, colorful prints of paintings that had never been reproduced before. I didn't know if I had done the right thing; I didn't know how much Jess could make out when she was reading these days. But the pictures were really big and bright and clear, and I hoped that on a good day, she'd be able to make them out. I was turning to leave when the gray-haired lady stopped me.

"You're Suzanne, Jessica's friend?" she asked.

I nodded.

"I'm Ms. McGehan," she said warmly. Her voice sounded like music. "I'm a live-in nurse here at Hope House. It was lovely of you to stop by on Jessica's birthday."

"Do you know Jessica?" I asked. I realize it was a stupid question, but it was the first thing that came into my head.

"Of course I know Jessica!" she said. "Everyone knows Jessica. Isn't that right, children?"

They all shouted their agreement. That's

when I took my first really good look at them. One little boy, a tousled blond, couldn't have been more than five. He was missing a leg; a metal brace extended from his knee to the floor. But it looked like he was getting around pretty well on it. Another little boy—about seven, I'd say—had curly red hair and freckles, and looked like a little elf. He was a little pale, but full of good spirits. There was a little girl, too. She must have been a little older, eight or nine maybe, and she was wearing a baseball cap.

As sweet and cheerful as the kids looked, I suddenly wanted to get out of there as fast as I could. "Will you tell Jessica I said hello?" I turned toward the door. "Nice to meet you, Ms. McGehan."

"Now, hold on," she said. "Didn't you come to see the birthday girl?"

I decided to level with her. "Ms. McGehan," I said, "I don't know if you know what's been going on with Jessica, but she doesn't want to see me. I know that."

"I do know about that," she said. She smiled. "But I didn't ask if *she* wanted to see *you*. I asked if *you* wanted to see *her*. Those are two different things, don't you agree?"

"Yes, but—"

"Suzanne, I don't think you understand what

I'm talking about." She managed to convince the other kids to run along, and patted me on the shoulder. "Come along, darlin'."

A few minutes later, Ms. McGehan and I were settled in the sun room sipping steaming mugs of hot chocolate that a woman named Mrs. Brady had brought us from the kitchen.

"I'll bet your friend Jessica must have really been something before all this came upon her," Ms. McGehan murmured almost absent-mindedly.

"Was? Jessica *is* really something!" I said indignantly. I couldn't help it—the words just came to me.

"That's the spirit!" she exclaimed, clapping her hands together. "I was just testing you," she added mischievously. "I wanted to make sure you had the right stuff." She leaned forward and looked at me seriously. "I work with a lot of sick children here, Suzanne. And some of them, well, just from looking at them, you wouldn't know a thing was wrong. Now, that's not the case with your friend Jessica. She's got something that she can't hide anymore."

"Yes, I know."

"I know you do, Suzanne. But Jessica is just starting to get used to that idea, and that's making a big difference."

"How do you know? How can you tell?"

"Oh, it's not important how I can tell. You can see for yourself. See those double doors over there, the glass ones with the yellow lacy curtains?"

"Yes?"

"Well, those doors lead to the playroom. Jessica is in there right now. She may not be ready to see you yet, but there's not a reason in the world why you can't see her."

"But what's Jessica doing in the playroom, anyway?"

"Go look for yourself if you'd like. Just be quiet, all right, dear?"

I tiptoed over to the doors, which were slightly open, and very slowly pulled back the curtain.

She was sitting at one of those miniature round tables—you remember the kind, from kindergarten—with her back to me. Jess was way too big for those little kids' chairs, of course. With her feet planted on the floor, her knees came up almost to her chest. She had her arms wrapped around her knees and was hugging them to her chest. I smiled when I realized she was wearing her wonderful sarong skirt from the party last fall, but now with a big, bulky corn-colored sweater.

There were three little kids at the table with her. I recognized the little redheaded boy from the hall. He must have found his way there while Ms. McGehan and I were in the sun room. I was close enough to them that I could hear what was going on.

"Okay, you guys," Jessica was saying. "Everybody close their eyes."

The three kids dutifully obeyed.

"Okay, Michelle, where are you going to take us?"

A little black girl, squinting purposefully to keep her eyes closed, answered, "Alaska! We're in Alaska!"

"Alaska," repeated Jessica. "I feel cold already. Brrrrrrrrrr!"

The kids laughed.

"Now, remember, Michelle, someday I may not be able to see it at all. So you have to tell me what it's like."

"Snow everywhere," said Michelle in her high-pitched little voice. "And ice! Big chunks of ice, tall as mountains!"

"Oh, neat. What else? Anybody?"

"Me, me! I want to say!"

"Okay, Alex, your turn."

The little redhead leapt out of his seat. "Eskimos and sleds! I want to take us on a ride!"

"Wonderful idea," Jessica said. "A dogsled ride. Everybody ready? Alex, you lead the way."

"Over there!" Alex called, pointing across the room.

"Wait a sec, Alex," Jess said. "Did you forget?"

"Oh, yeah, that's right," the little boy exclaimed. He came around the table, extended his arm again, and placed Jessica's hand on it so she could feel the direction.

"I got it, I think," Jessica said. "Over by the building blocks near the window?"

"Yeah," Michelle piped in. "That's our igloo, and the sled is right there!"

"Okay, I'll meet you there."

Michelle and the other little girl clambered out of their chairs and followed Alex over to the building blocks.

Jessica stood up now too. For the first time, I noticed the slender white cane hooked around the back of her chair. She started to pick it up, then let it go. I could tell she was being careful, but she managed to make her way across the room without it. It was slow going, and she had to let her fingers graze the surface of a table here, the back of a chair there, to find her bearings. But she did it!

I let the curtain drop, and walked back

across the room to Ms. McGehan. "She's really working hard, isn't she?" I said, feeling tears well up in my eyes.

"Harder than she's ever had to work in her life," Ms. McGehan said. "And where were they going today? Swimming in the Mississippi? Disneyland? A desert island?"

"Alaska."

"Might as well have stayed home," she said merrily, pointing out the window. It had started snowing again. Ms. McGehan sighed. "It warms the heart to see how wonderful she is with the little ones. And them with her." She went on to tell me how a little girl named Adrienne, who was born blind, had been helping Jessica learn Braille.

"It's all happened so fast," I said with a sigh. "It seems like her eyes have gotten so much worse so fast."

"Yes, I know love. But her eyes had been going bad for a while. And since she's come to stay with us, she's stopped hiding it. It took time, though. She wants so badly to do everything perfectly. And when you're losing your eyesight, you just can't make those demands on yourself."

We were quiet for a minute.

"And now, love?"

128

"Huh?"

"What do you want to do now, Suzanne?"

"I don't know what I can do." I looked at her carefully. "Anyway," I said, gulping, "I'm just glad I got the chance to see how she's doing for myself. Thanks, Ms. McGehan."

She sucked in her breath. "Oh my," she whispered.

The door from the playroom had opened. The kids were spilling into the sun room, Jessica among them.

"What a great ride, Alex," Jessica was saying. "We must do it again sometime."

The little boy beamed. "When, Jessica?"

She laughed. "Hey, you're going to wear me out completely. Maybe later this afternoon. Right now, I have a Braille lesson with Adrienne. You want to help me find her?"

"Sure," exclaimed the little boy. Then he spotted us. "Ms. McGehan and your friend can come too," he said.

Jess had pulled out her eyeglasses from her pocket, put them on, and was peering in my direction.

"Can we all go look for Adrienne before I have my dialysis?" Alex said, wheedling Ms. McGehan. "Can we, can we, can we?"

Ms. McGehan gave the little boy a hug,

looking up at Jess and me. "No, I don't think so, sweetie. You come along with me now, and let's leave the two friends to catch up."

Before I could stop her, she had disappeared with Alex. Now it was just Jessica and me, standing at opposite ends of the room.

"What are you doing here, Suzanne?" Jess's voice was flat.

"Jess," I said. "I'm sorry. I know you don't want me around. I was just leaving." But it was like my feet were stuck to the ground. I couldn't move.

She didn't move either. "How long have you been here? Were you watching me in there?" Now her voice was icy.

"Yes."

"Pretty pathetic, huh?"

"No, I don't think so. I don't think so at all. It looks like you're doing really great, Jess."

"You were always my biggest fan." She laughed disparagingly.

"I still am," I said quietly.

"I need a lot of help to get around, to do things. I'm pretty slow, did you notice?"

"Yeah."

"I'll never be like I was."

"I know."

"Had to see for yourself, huh? Satisfied?"

"Jess, I'm leaving now, okay?"

"Can't take it, huh?"

"It's hard," I admitted. "But I think I can take it if you can."

"I can't, Suzanne."

I picked up my bag and started heading for the door.

"Suzanne." Jess's voice stopped me. It was soft. Barely a whisper. "Wait a minute. Come over here."

"No," I said quietly, trying not to cry. "I can't, Jess. I'm sorry. I can't."

"Okay, I understand." Her voice went from soft to hard. "Nice of you to drop by anyway," she said harshly.

"Wait, let me finish," I said. "I won't come over there. I can't do it alone. But I'll meet you halfway."

Jessica stood still for a minute. It seemed like a century to me. Then she put out her cane and took a small, wobbly step. Then another. Then another.

I ran toward her and put my arms around her. She put her arms around me and we held each other tight, both of us crying.

11

The next week, Jessica returned to school, with her heavy glasses and white cane. But there was one place that she avoided like the plague: the art studio.

"No time," she said whenever I brought it up. "I've got to be at Hope House every day by four. I've got tons of work to catch up on."

But I continued to pester her about it.

"You don't get it, do you?" she finally said. "I don't *want* to go back to the art studio."

Ms. Skylar was bugging her about it too. "Just got a new shipment of clay, Jessica," she said one day, sitting down next to us in the cafeteria. "I thought you might like to stop in and play around with it."

"No, thanks."

"But you really enjoyed working with clay

last year in middle school," Ms. Skylar prompted.

"Yeah, Jess, you made some pretty good pots," I said.

"Thanks," she said distractedly, picking at her fingernails.

"Jessica," Ms. Skylar said. "We all know you can't do everything that you once did. But clay is a wonderful medium for you now. Why don't you give it a try?"

"Art therapy, huh?" cracked Jessica. "I know, they do it over at Hope House too. Why don't I make some little pot holders? Blind people are good at that."

"I didn't mean it that way, and you know it," Ms. Skylar said. "You're too good an artist to give up now, Jessica. You still have a good deal of eyesight left, and even when you don't—"

"Look, Ms. Skylar, maybe it's you who should give up. Maybe it would just make you feel better if I came back to the art studio. Don't get me wrong, I appreciate everything you've done for me, but—"

"Okay, Jessica," Ms. Skylar said as she got up. "But if you change your mind—"

"I won't," Jess said, but the edge had dropped out of her voice. "Don't worry, Ms.

Skylar, it's okay the way it is. Really."

"Suzanne, I hate to ask you, but could you bus it over to Hope House with me after school?" Jess asked one afternoon later that week. "It's kind of cloudy today; I think I could use the help. Ms. McGehan was going to come by to get me, but she's got to stop at the hospital. Maybe you could even hang around and play with the kids with me for a while."

"Good girl!" I clapped her on the back. "You're getting better at that. I think that's the first time you asked for help without completely choking."

Then a totally weird thing happened.

Marc Williams, the same Marc Williams who had barely spoken to Jessica in weeks, came over and asked if he could come to Hope House with us.

Jess went pale. "Uh, I don't know, Marc. Why would you want to go over there? I mean . . ."

She was getting all flustered. I wanted to do something to help, but I didn't know what.

"Maybe some other time," she said finally.

"Listen," he said, leaning over the table and putting his face close to hers. "Give me another

135

chance. Please. I know I've been acting like a total jerk. But it would mean a lot to me if you let me come. It really would."

"Hello, Ms. McGehan."

"Hello there, love," she sang out.

Jess and Marc hadn't even made it into the hallway before a handful of little kids had gathered around her.

"Hold on, hold on, you guys," Jessica was panting. "Give me a chance to get my coat off."

"Jessica, thank goodness you're here," Ms. McGehan said. "Dr. Ambrose called; she's going to be late today. Andrea Shepherd isn't feeling well, and these little ones are going gaga today. Do you think you and your friends can do something with them until Dr. Ambrose gets here?"

"Sure thing," said Jess.

We spent the next half hour in the rec room with Alex, Michelle, and the other little girl, whose name I learned was Jennifer. Both the little girls had fallen deeply, hopelessly in love with Marc within the first fifteen minutes.

We went traveling—to a beach in Hawaii, up to the moon in a rocket, under the sewers with the Ninja Turtles. Occasionally I'd catch Michelle peeking through her fingers to make sure Marc was coming along too.

At first I was worried about Marc. How he'd handle being in Hope House. But after the first few minutes, he really seemed to be doing okay.

But you can't keep little kids playing one game for long. They get restless. "How about something to drink?" Jessica suggested.

"Yeah!" screamed Alex, sprinting out of the room. When we got there he was already at the refrigerator, pulling out a carton of orange juice from the bottom shelf.

"You're lucky this is Mrs. Brady's morning off," Jessica said. "She cooks for all of us," she explained to Marc and me, "and she doesn't like these little monkeys fooling around in her kitchen."

Marc pulled out a ladder-back chair from the big round kitchen table, straddled it backwards, rested his chin on the top slat, and watched Jessica as she methodically moved around the kitchen, finding cups and napkins and depositing them carefully on the tabletop. Michelle, Jennifer, and Alex finished their juice in a second, and started demanding more games.

"Whew, I'm really beat from all that traveling, you guys. Can you give us a little break?" Jessica said.

I was surprised at how obligingly the kids scooted out of the kitchen. I guess Michelle and Jennifer, in particular, didn't want to do anything that might threaten their relationship with their new heartthrob.

There must have been something about the mood right then that made Marc ask quietly, "How much can you actually see, Jess? What's it like?"

"Oh, it's not as bad as you might think. Dr. Ambrose says she thinks the worst part is all the straining I do. I can see pretty much in the light, the general outlines of things, but it's all kind of blurry."

"Can you see my face?" he asked.

"Yeah, sort of. I mean, I can see where your face is, but I can't see what you're doing with it, if you know what I mean. Dr. Ambrose says I should stop straining to see things better by squinting."

"Like you're doing now?"

"Oh, am I?" She laughed self-consciously. "Yeah, I guess I am." I could tell she was trying to unfurrow her brow, but the effort to relax was only making the skin around her eyes wrinkle more.

"Stop squinting, Jess," he said gently. "I'll tell you what I'm doing. I'm smiling at you."

"Yeah, I kind of thought so. And I can hear it in your voice."

"It's gonna get worse though, huh?" he asked.

"Yes." There was a long pause, but it didn't feel uncomfortable. "But I'm not going to die, Marc. Suzanne told be about your sister. It's not going to be like that."

"Yeah, I know," he said. But I could see how much the memory hurt him.

We all sat there in silence for a while, staring at each other. I caught Marc's eye and he smiled. Jess saw it too. I know she did. It was kind of a sad little smile, but it made me know everything was going to be okay.

"Dr. Ambrose says I might even need to get a Seeing Eye dog at some point. I'm kind of looking forward to that, believe it or not." She shrugged her shoulders and smiled. "If I get a dog, what do you think I should call him?"

"Or her," I said. "Don't be sexist, Jess."

"Oh, you're right. All right, what about him or her?"

"Frida," Marc said quietly.

"What?"

"Frida. You know, like the movie we saw. That artist. The one who had the terrible accident but didn't give up."

It seemed like about a hundred expressions, a hundred emotions, passed across Jessica's face. A hundred different shades of pain and hurt and loss all mixed up together. Jessica sank into a chair. "Forget it, Marc. I know what you're going to say; Suzanne's been after me about it too. It seems like everyone is."

"But you were so good, Jessica," Marc said. "How can you give it up?"

"*Were*," Jessica repeated emphatically. "That's the key word."

"No. That's not true," He said. "You've got to stop worrying and feeling sorry for yourself. You've got to try to—" He stopped, checking himself.

Jessica ran her hand across her forehead wearily, jiggling her thick glasses a bit in the process. "It seems like everyone has their theory about what Jessica should or shouldn't be doing. And they're never satisfied until they get it off their chest. Go ahead, Marc. Your turn."

"Listen, Jessica," he began haltingly, "you're a wonderful artist. Not were. Are. It's not just what you do that makes you an artist. It's who you are. It kills me to see you giving that up."

Jessica slammed her fist down on the table.

"Don't I get a little credit for anything? Don't I get a little credit for knowing what I can and can't do?"

Marc ignored her outburst. "Jessica, do you still want to make art?"

"Yes!" Jessica said so loudly it frightened me. "Yes, of course I do! It's all I've ever wanted to do!"

I hadn't seen Jessica even shed a tear since that day we made up in the sun room. And this time it was different. She was shaking. "Why doesn't anyone get it? How can I be an artist if I can barely see?" She lay down her head on the table and started sobbing. Really sobbing. Marc moved closer to her, and put his arm around her shoulders. But he didn't try to stop her, and neither did I.

"Your art was never about seeing, Jess," I said slowly and very softly. "It was about feeling. And you don't feel with your eyes." I was crying now too. "You feel with your heart."

Jessica's sobs had diminished into little gasps. Nobody said anything for a long time. Then Marc stood up.

"I'm going to go now, Jess. I horned in this afternoon because I wanted to be with you again, but that was selfish. I acted like a jerk, and I'm sorry. It's up to you to decide if you want to have anything to do with me after this. But at least I got to say what I think."

Jessica didn't try to stop him. Neither did I.

At the kitchen door, Marc turned again. "But remember," he said. "Frida. For Frida Kahlo."

12

"Psssst! Marc!"

"Shhh." Marc poked his head out from the art studio. "You'll disturb her," he said.

"How's she doing in there? I can't believe she won't let me in to see!"

"She wants to surprise you, you know that."

"But it's not fair," I whined. "She lets you see. How come you're the only one?"

Marc slipped out the door and quietly closed it behind him. "You know why. She thinks you'll be too easy on her. She knows I'm a jerk"—he laughed—"therefore, I rate visiting privileges."

"I've definitely got my monster side too," I insisted.

"You don't have to tell *me* that," Marc said, laughing.

"But listen, when's she coming out of there?" I pressed. "Gym class was over ten minutes ago, and I've got an appointment to set her up in geography class."

That's how we worked it now. Marc or I or Paul, or one of her other friends, would take turns accompanying Jess to her classes, making sure that everything was set up in each room for her the way she needed.

But since she'd gone back into the studio, it was almost impossible to tear her out. "Making up for lost time," she told me. She was in there every chance she got. And since Jess couldn't take gym classes with us anymore, she used the time in the studio.

"Okay." Marc poked his head in the door again. "Jess, clean up," he called. "It's time for your favorite subject."

We both heard Jess's melodramatic groan, and laughed.

Of course, it wasn't as bad as all that anymore. Mr. Vickers had realized that Jess's problems in geography had come from not being able to see the maps well enough. He'd ordered these special desk maps for her from the Retinitis Pigmentosa Foundation. That organization had been great—they had all kinds of information about special programs and materials for the visually impaired.

"It doesn't make geography class any less boring," Jess had quipped, "but at least it makes it bearable."

"Okay, take me to my doom," Jess said, emerging from the studio.

Marc and I exchanged glances.

"Something's wrong, huh?" asked Jess, wrinkling her brow. "Okay, where? On my nose?"

"Yeah," I said, drawing out the word with my voice going up at the end.

"In my hair, too?"

"Uh-huh," said Marc.

"Okay, guys, enough," she pouted. "Just tell me where the darn clay is so I can wash it off."

"Try everywhere," I suggested.

"You need more than a sink, you need a shower!" Marc said.

"Very funny, you guys," Jess said. "I'd better wash it off, then. I guess I have no choice but to go back into the studio," she said mischievously, slipping back through the door and slamming it behind her. "I'll be finished in a second," she called.

"I can't tell you how many times I've heard that line, " I told Marc as he disappeared inside the studio with Jess.

* * *

Emergency call at 7:05 P.M. on Friday, March 12, from Hope House.

"Suzanne," Jessica gasped hoarsely. "It's horrible, it's horrible. I know my sculpture is horrible. I don't know why I put it in the contest."

"Now calm down; it can't be as bad as you think."

"Oh yes it can," she insisted. "You don't know, you haven't seen it."

I didn't want to point out that neither had she, because I understood that was precisely the problem. I just knew I had to calm her down. I had to think fast.

"What does Marc think? He's seen it."

"Oh, what does it matter? You're the only one I really trust."

I was surprised. "I am?"

Now she sounded surprised. "Well, of course, Suzanne, you know that. Why do you think you're my best friend?"

"I don't know. Sometimes I wonder."

"Su-za-anne, can we *please* get back to my problem? My piece is a mess, I tried really hard, but I know it's a mess! It's so awful, Suzanne, and I—"

"Shhh," I demanded. "Let me think for a minute." I thought. I didn't come up with much. Except with the realization that maybe

I'd been floating along in a bubble too for the last couple of weeks. We all wanted to believe that if Jess set her mind to making art again, she could do it as well as she always had. But was that realistic? My bubble came crashing to earth. I grabbed at the first thing that came into my head.

"Jess, you have other things in the show besides that sculpture, right? Things you made before. The judges aren't going to make their decision on just one piece."

Jess had gotten hold of herself now. "Oh, Suzanne, it's not about the contest anymore. After all, what could it possibly do for me to visit museums and galleries in New York now?"

I hadn't thought about that.

"It was just about—well, it was just about *trying*. Oh, I don't know how to explain it."

"Listen, Jess, that's what you did," I said firmly. "You tried. Now you walk in there with your head held high, and be proud of yourself."

"Okay," she said weakly. "I guess I have no choice. But I can't wait till this thing is over."

"Well, Jess, you know what they say. Every horrible experience is a learning experience."

"Yeah. But if I have one more learning experience this year, I swear I'm gonna kill myself."

* * *

Marc and Paul and I made a beeline for Jessica when she walked through the cafeteria door with my folks and her dad.

It was one of her bad nights, I could tell. She was using her cane, and her special night-vision aid, this little contraption about the size of a beeper that fit discreetly in her hand.

"Okay, guys, let's get this over with," she said.

Together we walked to the front of the cafeteria, where there were round tables set up around a podium for the ceremony. With my parents and her dad, we filled one of the tables.

Marc was holding both my hand and Jess's under the table. "What does it look like?" Jess asked.

"Pretty good, pretty good," I replied. "There's some nice stuff in here."

"Tell me about it."

I did, describing each piece as well as I could, ending with Jorie Cambell's watercolors. "They're good, Jess, especially the one with the—what do you call them—those purple flowers?"

"Asters."

"Yeah, and she's put them in some really nice frames."

"Okay, give me the bad news. What about my work?"

"It's right next to them. Remember the painting you did last September? It looks fantastic." Jess squinted in that direction.

"Yeah, I can make it out," she said. "It's *not* bad, is it?"

"Not bad at all. And those prints you did in October are right beside it; they look great!"

"But what about the sculpture?"

That was the funny thing. It was on a pedestal right next to her other stuff. "Actually, the canvas is still over it."

Rather than being upset, Jess seemed relieved. "Ms. Skylar was in here with them when they were doing the judging. Maybe when she saw what a mess it was, and did that for me to save me the embarrassment."

"Maybe. But remember what we discussed on the phone. This was all about trying, not winning, right?"

"That's right," said Jessica. "I've got nothing to be ashamed of, right?"

Ms. Skylar tapped the microphone. "Ladies and gentlemen," she began. "May I have your attention." First Ms. Skylar introduced the judges. There were three of them. The first was the associate editor from the art magazine that was sponsoring the contest. The second was a curator of a museum in New York, and the third was an artist—Jessica gasped when she heard the name, but it didn't mean anything to me, of course.

Then the associate editor got up and made a short speech about the contest, about the "high quality" of the work at Somerset in particular, and about how it was so hard to judge because each student was really a winner—the standard rap that grown-ups give you whenever there's a contest. Of course, it was particularly true in Jessica's case, so I kept squeezing her hand meaningfully.

"And now it is my pleasure to announce the winners. We have two honorable mentions tonight before we get to the grand prize. They are Sam Wendover, for his outstanding photography, and Lavinia Smith, for her excellent collages." Everyone clapped appreciatively as Sam and Lavinia came to the podium to accept their honorable mention certificates.

"And I invite you to look for their work after the ceremony," the associate editor continued after they had returned to their seats. "And to look at all the work that's here tonight by Somerset High's exceptional student artists." Then he cleared his throat.

Okay, this was it. The grand prize. It could only be Jessica or Jorie Cambell for her watercolors, we all knew that. And if Jess was right—if Ms. Skylar really had convinced the judges not to factor in Jess's sculpture—then she still had a chance.

"Well, in this case, we'd rather show you than tell you," the editor said. He started heading over toward the west wall. But it was impossible to tell if he was going toward Jessica's or Jorie's work.

"You're a winner, Jess, you're a winner," I heard Marc whispering in her ear.

"Where's the judge?" asked Jess. "I can't see."

I was afraid to speak, afraid I'd be wrong.

"The grand-prize winner," said the editor, sweeping his hand across the wall, "is Jessica Elliot!"

A roar went up at our table.

"You did it, Jess, you did it!" I screamed.

Jessica was smiling, but a small tear was sliding out of the side of her right eye. "Well, I used to be good," she whispered. "At least I *used* to be good."

The audience was still applauding. Paul came around the table to where Marc and I were pushing her to her feet. The applause grew louder. But the judge was raising his hand to stop us.

I was annoyed. Let my friend have her full moment of glory.

"Excuse me," he was saying, "excuse me." When we quieted a bit, he went on. "All the judges agreed that Ms. Elliot's work from the beginning of the semester was superb. But the piece that impressed us the most you haven't even seen yet."

The whole room went quiet as he lifted off the cloth.

I know I'll never find the words to describe what I felt at that moment. Because Jessica's sculpture—well, it was a sculpture of *me*. I knew that in a second. But the thing was, it was really of me and Jessica at the same time. It was my high cheekbones and my squarish jaw and wide mouth and my wavy hair falling over my forehead, even though things were a little off kilter. It was a little awkward, but it was also beautiful, I knew it was. Not because I'm beautiful. For the first time, I guess, I saw myself through Jessica's eyes. Well, not her eyes exactly, but her feelings.

It had the curve of my brow over my eyes, the fullness of my lips. But all the pain and fears Jessica had had to face in the last year were in that portrait of me. It was in the tentative trace of her fingers along the clay in some places and the rough edges in other places, the mistakes that weren't mistakes because you could tell that was where Jess had to give up on sense and rely on instinct.

I couldn't move. I couldn't speak.

A ripple of applause started up again and became a wave. It washed over us as Jess put her arms around me and we held each other tight.

Then I was crying. Why shouldn't I be?

"Jess, it's perfect," I said.